Keith turned to me. "The name Roanna Aylmer sound familiar to you?"

I blinked. It was the last name I expected to hear. I saw her in my mind's eye—tall, dark-haired, her face reflecting a rebellious arrogance I'd found irresistible. "You know it does," I said.

"Seen her lately?"

"Of course not. I'm forbidden to."

Keith's smile was cynical. "And you always obey orders, Denise, don't you?"

"I try."

Cynthia's lips twitched. She knew me well.

"So what's with Roanna Aylmer?" I said casually.

"She's coming here today. I'd like both of you to sit in on the meeting. My office at three."

The sudden realization I was about to see Roanna again had jolted me. My face felt hot. I hoped I wasn't visibly blushing.

I became aware that Keith was frowning at me. "Is there some problem, Denise?"

"No problem."

"Because I'm quite aware you and Ms. Aylmer have—how shall I put it—some history together. She claims to have a lead to Righteous Scourge. I remind you, Denise, that she was never cleared of espionage. There was simply not enough concrete evidence against her. She could be playing a double game here. I'm relying on you to find out if she is."

Visit

Bella Books

at

BellaBooks.com

or call our toll-free number

1-800-729-4992

Murder at Random

Claire McNab

Bella
BOOKS

2006

Bella Books, Inc.
P.O. Box 10543
Tallahassee, FL 32302

Printed in the United States of America on acid-free paper
First Edition

Editor: Anna Chinappi
Cover designer: Sandy Knowles

ISBN 1-59493-047-3

For Sheila

Acknowledgments

My gratitude to Kevin Grant for technical information. As always, I appreciate all the work my editor Anna Chinappi does. Thank you, Anna. And thanks also to Ruth Stanley, Pamela Berard and Therese Szymanski at Bella Books.

About the Author

CLAIRE MCNAB is the author of fifteen Detective Inspector Carol Ashton mysteries: *Lessons in Murder, Fatal Reunion, Death Down Under, Cop Out, Dead Certain, Body Guard, Double Bluff, Inner Circle, Chain Letter, Past Due, Set Up, Under Suspicion, Death Club, Accidental Murder* and *Blood Link*. She has written two romances, *Under the Southern Cross* and *Silent Heart*, and has co-authored a self-help book, *The Loving Lesbian*, with Sharon Gedan. She is the author of four Denise Cleever thrillers, *Murder Undercover, Death Understood, Out of Sight*, and *Recognition Factor*.

An Australian now living permanently in Los Angeles, she teaches fiction writing in the UCLA Extension Writers' Program. She makes it a point to return once a year to Australia to refresh her Aussie accent.

CHAPTER ONE

This morning there'd been another sniper attack, this time in suburban Sydney. The victim was a middle-aged stockbroker, standing on Milson's Point railway station with a crowd of other commuters waiting for the 8:05 train to the city. The sniper had been on the roof of an adjacent multi-storied building. The stockbroker had died instantly from a clean hit, right in the center of his forehead. In the mad scramble to escape further shots, a schoolgirl had fallen headfirst down the stairs to the platform and broken her neck.

At the Australian Security Intelligence Organization headquarters in Canberra, Australia's federal capital, 300 kilometers southwest of Sydney, the news was received with grim resignation. It had been six days since the last sniper strike, and after the first one, all the subsequent attacks had been at intervals of five to seven days.

Cynthia and I both worked for the ASIO. She was my control when I was undercover in the field, and I'd been summoned to her office for one of our last face-to-face meetings before I assumed my new identity.

I always found it a rather startling room. No standard-issue government furnishings for Cynthia. Strange, contorted sculptures of vaguely human shapes sat in the corners, holding down a rectangular grass-green rug. The walls held paintings that were mostly frantic swirls of luminescent rainbow colors. Cynthia's clothing matched the room—odd outfits in bright shades that would appear ridiculous on most people but somehow managed to look just right on her.

Cynthia never merely sat on chairs, but perched on them in yoga-like poses. She was so supple, I imagined she could have had a career as a contortionist had she not decided on intelligence as a profession.

She was very attractive, in her own strange way. At least I found her so. Maybe it had something to do with the fact that Cynthia was an enigma to me. I had only the sketchiest information about her private life, and I'd never liked to probe too obviously as I was pretty sure she'd object. I valued our working relationship too much to jeopardize it.

Sunlight lancing through the window lit up Cynthia's mobile face. She had a charming, crooked smile, and was displaying it now, as she observed, "I see you're working on looking the part of urban terrorism expert. I like the no-nonsense specs. Nice touch."

I took off the severe black frames. Since I'd had laser surgery, I no longer needed contact lenses or spectacles, so these were plain glass. "How about the hair?" I asked. My usual streaked blond now tended towards mousy brown.

"Boring hairstyle, boring color," she said. "Perfect."

Cynthia's hair was the antithesis of mine, spiky and often an extraordinary color. Today it was a deep burgundy.

"In contrast, Cynthia, you have an interesting hairstyle, arresting color," I remarked.

"Courtney," she said. "Get the name straight, Denise."

"That would be Ann, thank you, Courtney. Ann Meadows, actually."

She grinned at me. "Touché."

Cynthia assumed a different name for each new assignment. Once the planning was underway, for practice we were always supposed to refer to each other by our pseudonyms, even when at ASIO headquarters.

"I much prefer the name you used on my last job," I said. "Zena was more you. Courtney doesn't have the same ring to it."

This was very true. I could never tell her, of course, but when she'd been Zena, my long unrequited, not-quite-serious yearning for Cynthia had led to some quite spectacular warrior-princess fantasies.

"Ann suits you," she said. "It's brisk, plain, down-to-earth. Exactly what one would want a consultant on terrorism to be."

This was to be my new undercover role—expert in urban terrorism. I was part of a concentrated effort by all the Australian intelligence agencies and the Australian Federal Police to track down an organization that called itself Righteous Scourge.

Three months earlier, the name had been entirely unknown to the intelligence community. Then ASIO had been alerted to the existence of a new terrorist Web site calling itself Righteous Scourge, and had already added it to the long list of sites under constant monitoring, when the first public mention of the group was made on Josiah Lyttle's extremely popular radio program.

I'd never been part of Lyttle's audience. I didn't share his particularly virulent, ultra-conservative beliefs, but I'd later listened to the radio station's recording of the session.

Josiah Lyttle's high-pitched, nasal voice had launched into the topic with frothing-at-the-mouth rhetoric. "Do you want your loved ones to suffer agonizing deaths at the hands of pitiless terrorists? Could you bear to see the tender bodies of your children shredded by nail-filled bombs? Can you visualize their contorted faces as they choke on sarin gas, or die horribly from smallpox or anthrax?"

He paused, apparently for his listeners to reflect that no, they didn't, and then he was off again. "The lefties and the tree-huggers and the deviants wring their lily-white hands, bleating about privacy rights and individual rights and homo rights and killing-unborn-baby rights, while the threat to our national security and our God-given way of life grows day by day. Wake up! We're under attack, people! A case in point—and you hear it here exclusively on my program—is a repellent, vicious Web site that calls itself Righteous Scourge. Take a look at it, people! While the radical left is moaning about loss of freedoms, sites like this are inciting wholesale slaughter of innocents! More in a moment . . ."

The program broke for a set of commercials. I'd said to my trainer, who'd been listening to it with me, "Lyttle's done the Righteous Scourge people a big favor. You can't buy that kind of publicity."

"You're right, of course, but no link's been found. And believe me, we've looked for it."

The combined might of Australia's intelligence organizations, plus help from Britain and America, still had produced no firm evidence of links to anyone or anything. Three months after the Web site had appeared we were essentially in the same state of ignorance.

"Am I interrupting?" Keith Francis, director of covert surveillance and officially my boss, put his long nose through Cynthia's door. He didn't wait for an answer but came right in, seized a chair, turned it around and sat down with his arms resting along the back.

His narrow nose was matched by his thin face, skinny limbs and bony hands. Any weight Keith put on went straight to his belly. If he'd been a woman, I'd have assumed he was in the last weeks of pregnancy.

I was quite fond of Keith, although he could be quite a stickler for rules and regulations, and I had a tendency to bend them a little—sometimes a lot—and this had led to friction between us in the past.

Cynthia was giving him her characteristic interrogative look. One eyebrow went up, and almost like a counterweight, the corners of her mouth went down. "Something's happened?"

"You could say that." He turned to me. "The name Roanna Aylmer sound familiar to you?"

I blinked. It was the last name I expected to hear. I saw her in my mind's eye—tall, dark-haired, her face reflecting a rebellious arrogance I'd found irresistible. "You know it does," I said.

"Seen her lately?"

"Of course not. I'm forbidden to."

Keith's smile was cynical. "And you always obey orders, Denise, don't you?"

"I try."

Cynthia's lips twitched. She knew me well.

I'd fallen hard for Roanna while playing an undercover role

to unmask the Aylmer family as traitors and murderers. Three of them were presently serving life sentences, but Roanna remained free, as there had been no direct evidence to connect her to the crimes. Even though she'd repudiated her family and been a witness against them, she was still regarded as a security risk, so there was no way I, working for ASIO, could have any personal contact with her.

At first, this hadn't stopped me, and we'd had passionate, clandestine meetings. However, as the months passed, two things combined to make our relationship untenable. First, I wasn't willing to give up my career and therefore had the constant fear that ASIO would discover what I was doing. Second, Roanna had taken over the running of the family's tropical resort near the Great Barrier Reef and could spend very little time away from the island.

"So what's with Roanna Aylmer?" I said casually.

"She's coming here today. I'd like both of you to sit in on the meeting. My office at three."

The sudden realization I was about to see Roanna again was a jolt. My face felt hot. I hoped I wasn't visibly blushing.

I became aware that Keith was frowning at me. "Is there some problem, Denise?"

"No problem."

"Because I'm quite aware you and Ms. Aylmer have—how shall I put it—some history together."

Cynthia's mouth tightened. "On that assignment, Denise's instructions explicitly included infiltrating the Aylmer family by any means available."

I glanced at her, surprised she was defending me. She didn't meet my eyes.

Keith gave an ironic chuckle. "Rarely have instructions been so enthusiastically followed by an agent in the field."

I gave a nonchalant shrug, not sure if he knew I'd continued the relationship for some time after the assignment had ended.

All amusement abruptly left Keith's face. "Roanna Aylmer claims to have a lead to Righteous Scourge. I remind you, Denise, that she was never cleared of espionage. There was simply not enough concrete evidence against her. She could be playing a double game here. I'm relying on you to find out if she is."

CHAPTER TWO

After Josiah Lyttle's mention of the Web site inciting violence against citizens, newspapers were the first in the general
media to pick up the story. I recalled seeing the first, relatively
mild headline:

AMATEUR TERRORISM FOR HIRE?
WEB SITE PROMISES REWARDS FOR SUCCESSFUL
ATTACKS

The news article went on to quote the sliding scale of pay-
ments Righteous Scourge guaranteed to anyone who accomplished an attack brutally violent enough to attract wide
publicity. Full national exposure in the media was to be
rewarded with a bonus. International exposure doubled the
original payment. Initial rewards started at two hundred thou-

sand dollars, but a truly spectacular terrorist sortie with high casualties could net the perpetrator upward of a million dollars.

Once it was in print, television stations ran with the story, many networks choosing to treat it with a breathless sensationalism that even had one studio personality exclaiming, "Millions in deadly peril! How many must die in agony before the government acts?"

Soon thousands, and then hundreds of thousands attempted to log on to the Righteous Scourge Web site, until it was overwhelmed by sheer numbers and crashed. It was soon up again, available in several languages.

The Web site was a professional job, crisp and easy to read. The home page contained a parody of the famous, much-imitated British World War I recruiting poster, where the words "Your country needs YOU" appear under the image of a heavily-mustached Lord Kitchener, who is pointing a stern finger at the viewer.

In the Righteous Scourge version, the figure was a hazy silhouette. His hand, with its emphatic forefinger was in high relief, focusing attention on the words: RIGHTEOUS SCOURGE NEEDS YOU!

Scrolling down, the offer became explicit.

ARE YOU BRAVE ENOUGH TO TAKE THE CHANCE?
ARE YOU WILLING TO KILL FOR $$$?
Have you ever dreamed of getting even with those who oppress you? Now you can—and be paid $$$ for your revenge. Do you hate the hypocrites of society, the people who think they're better than you? The ones who put you down?
DESTROY THEM!
THIS IS NOT A JOKE
HATE PAYS

COLD HARD CASH IN ANY CURRENCY YOU
CHOOSE
OFF-SHORE BANKS PROTECT YOUR IDENTITY
TAX FREE!

All security services, including ASIO, treated the issue seriously. There was no guarantee the Web site really intended to
fund terrorist activity, but there were any number of unbalanced
individuals in society for whom the offer was likely to provide
an incitement to violence.

It immediately became obvious that whoever was behind
Righteous Scourge had employed experts to protect the Web
site from hackers. The host server was in a small island state,
implacably hostile toward the West, and the site itself was protected with sophisticated encryption protocols.

The Web site gave explicit directions to those seeking to
contact Righteous Scourge, urging them to go to cyber-cafes or
libraries to originate their messages and to use anonymous
mailers to protect their identities.

There was much discussion about whether to disrupt the
Web site by shutting it down using a virus in a denial-of-service
attack, similar to the process that had caused the site to crash
when huge numbers of people had tried to access it initially.
The general consensus was that it was better to leave the site in
operation, in the hopes that Righteous Scourge would eventually make a mistake and expose themselves to penetration. In
that event, backtracking the e-mail addresses of any potential
terrorist who'd contacted the Web site would be of great value.

Linguists had analyzed the language used, and had come to
the conclusion that the author of the text was almost certainly a
native English speaker, possibly Australian. This, of course, was
no indication of the nationality or ethnicity of the person or
persons behind the name.

Meanwhile, the media grappled with the question of how much weight to give the story. From the beginning, there had been no agreement over whether this was an elaborate hoax or a genuine attempt to induce individuals to commit terrorist acts. Comedians incorporated Righteous Scourge into their routines, columnists mused on the issue, politicians pontificated. The prime minister huffed indignantly—his standard response to matters that he perceived might be factors in the next election.

When, after three weeks, nothing had happened, both the government and the public lost interest in the issue. Righteous Scourge seemed destined to be yet another journalistic flash in the pan.

Then the killings began.

The first terrorist attack attributed to Righteous Scourge's solicitation to kill occurred exactly three weeks and two days after the Web site's existence had first been publicized in the media.

It was Saturday lunchtime at a large regional shopping mall in the suburban area of Adelaide, the state capital of South Australia. The mall's food hall was crowded with shoppers taking a break. The bomb, a crude homemade device, which nevertheless was horribly effective, had been hidden in a clump of artificial shrubbery in the center of a large area filled with tables and chairs, where food purchased from any of twenty outlets could be eaten in relative comfort.

Because there were many families shopping that day, the casualties included children. In the pandemonium that followed the explosion, several people were trampled. The final toll was eight dead, three of them children. Twenty-five were seriously injured, seven sustaining grave wounds.

The perpetrator of this carnage was anything but an accomplished terrorist. Film later taken from security cameras had picked up Trevor Ulrich, disguised as a cleaner with bucket and mop, furtively planting the bomb at six that morning, and his call to the police claiming responsibility for the attack had been recorded, so a voiceprint could be taken.

Ulrich was a loner, with rounded shoulders and a fat, doughy face. He had a burning resentment against any form of authority, so had never held a job for long. Until this particular Saturday, his criminal record had been a string of petty offences, none of them violent.

By the time Ulrich arrived at the international airport to start the journey he'd booked to the Cayman Islands, where his payment was presumably waiting in a personalized bank account, Righteous Scourge already had details of the mall bombing up on its Web site and was advising prospective contractors with similar ambitions: YOU CAN DO BETTER! It urged them to register by e-mail directly with the Web site for an opportunity to attain a similar cash payout to the one the Adelaide bomber was about to enjoy.

Ulrich, identified by a neighbor from his security camera appearance, which had been widely shown on television, was arrested without incident by Australian Federal Police at the airport before he had boarded his flight. He was taken to a special interrogation unit for questioning.

Expert grilling was hardly needed as Trevor Ulrich was proud of his achievement and pleased with the concentrated attention it had generated. With one step he'd gone from pathetic little lawbreaker to urban terrorist.

I'd seen the video of his interview. The most chilling thing about the man was that the slaughter and maiming of innocent people only interested him in terms of numbers. "Only eight dead?" he'd said to his interrogators, obviously unhappy the toll had not been higher. "But a lot badly injured?"

It hadn't been difficult to persuade Ulrich to describe the steps he'd taken to establish himself as Righteous Scourge's first successful terrorist for hire. On the interrogation tape, he'd smoothed his thinning hair and looked earnestly into the camera. "You're recording this? People will see it?"

Assured that many interested parties would view his interview, he settled back in his chair. "I heard about the Web site, and it sounded ideal. I'd been wanting to do something like this for some time . . ." His soft, white face had reflected his bitter anger. "It's not right, the way I've been treated. I've never had a chance. People always try to bring me down. They talk behind my back, spread lies, laugh at me. But I showed them, didn't I?"

It was almost immediately clear that apprehending the amateur terrorists like Trevor Ulrich would not help in the search for the shadowy figures behind Righteous Scourge. He'd followed the Web site's helpful advice on sending e-mails via a series of anonymous mailers to disguise the source of the message.

In a similar fashion, the series of e-mails from Righteous Scourge to Ulrich looking for details and dispensing instructions had been layered through a series of anonymous mailers until the trail was lost in an electronic sea.

The next morning's edition of Australia's new national newspaper *The Austral Trumpeter* had screamed in huge black letters:
TERRORISM FOR PAY NO JOKE
ADELAIDE BOMBER'S BLOOD MONEY IN OFF-SHORE BANK
WHO WILL BE NEXT?

The ambiguity of "Who Will Be Next?" hit me—was it the next victim or the next would-be terrorist?

Whether or not money had been actually deposited for Ulrich in a Cayman Islands' bank—inquiries were met with the expected refusal to reveal particulars for any client—it appeared that some potential mercenaries were convinced of Righteous Scourge's good faith, as two days later there was a second amateur terrorist attack.

This time it was a train derailment, and not nearly as effective as Ulrich's strike. The points had been manually switched on a busy rail route outside Melbourne, causing two trains to derail—one a half-empty passenger train, the other a freight train on a parallel line. No one was killed, but fifteen people sustained mild to serious injuries.

Alec O'Donnell, an ex-engineer with a long-standing grievance against the railways, was almost immediately arrested. He steadfastly denied having anything to do with the Web site, but he'd failed to follow directions to conceal his identity when e-mailing. A sweep of the hard drive of his personal computer soon revealed damning e-mails he'd believed deleted, including one to Righteous Scourge expressing his anxiety that he not be swindled out of his just reward.

Faced with this evidence, O'Donnell admitted he'd contacted Righteous Scourge to offer his services, and been asked to provide step-by-step details of his plans. Once his proposal had been accepted, it had been agreed between them that an effective railway accident with casualties would be worth a minimum payment of one hundred thousand dollars. A spectacular crash, with many lives lost, plus widespread media coverage, would triple this amount.

A third would-be terrorist was foiled when he made an almost laughably inept attempt to blow up one of the northern pylons of the Sydney Harbour Bridge. Spotted at midnight by a police patrol, Bert Smithy was doing his clumsy best to climb one of the sandstone pylons while struggling with the weight of a backpack full of sticks of dynamite.

Interrogated, he admitted that he'd told Righteous Scourge that he was an experienced demolition specialist—somewhat of an exaggeration, as his only experience with explosives had been blowing up tree stumps when clearing paddocks in the country.

Smithy declared with some pride that he'd been promised half a million dollars if such a famous landmark as the Sydney Harbour Bridge could be substantially damaged and traffic seriously disrupted. Relatively minor destruction would merit a smaller payment.

By this stage, many in the media were making disparaging remarks about the expertise of such unprofessional mercenaries, who'd been apprehended with apparently little effort by the authorities. Political cartoonists had fun drawing would-be terrorists ludicrously bungling attacks on various institutions and landmarks, including the Sydney Opera House, Ayres Rock and the Murray-Murrumbidgee river system. Alone among the newspapers, *The Austral Trumpeter* solemnly warned against complacency.

The mockery stopped when the anthrax mailings began.

CHAPTER THREE

Since the worldwide rise in international terrorism, law enforcement and intelligence organizations had been alert to the possibility that some form of biological weapon could be used against Australia's citizens. It was thought that anthrax would be one of the most likely agents, especially after the 2001 anthrax scare in the United States. There had only been five deaths, but worldwide publicity had been very effective in instilling in the ordinary person an almost irrational fear of the disease.

There was limited preventative action that could be taken ahead of time. Lacking a specific threat to take to the public, vague warnings would only have a short term effect. At least, if an attempt to spread anthrax through the mail occurred, plans were already in place to quarantine sorting hubs and post offices and to distribute antibiotics stockpiled at various medical centers to those at most risk of infection.

The attack, when it came, was well-coordinated. The plain envelopes had neatly typed addresses, and were sent to reporters, state and national politicians, various business and entertainment personalities and a selection of ordinary citizens. Bundles of envelopes were posted in every state, and wherever the initial mailing point, it was obvious they were all intended to arrive at their destinations in Monday's mail deliveries. Of course, given the various inefficiencies of the postal authorities, some letters arrived late, long after the alarm had been raised.

The envelopes each contained a single word typed on a white card—ANTHRAX—and an amount of white powder.

Immediately general panic ensued, fueled by the media, where horror stories detailing the stages of death by anthrax were the order of the day. Post offices were closed, mailrooms shut down, and the drug Cipro, one of the few effective treatments for anthrax, was so much in demand there were near riots at dispensing centers. On the street, the price of illicit Cipro tablets shot through the roof.

When the supposed anthrax was analyzed, and found to be merely talcum powder, the anger in the media was palpable, and headlines such as AUTHORITIES FOOLED BY HOAX ANTHRAX did not disguise the uncomfortable fact that the media itself had also been hoodwinked.

Amid the relief ordinary people felt that this was an elaborate practical joke, *The Austral Trumpeter* ran a banner headline on page one.

WHAT IF IT'S ANTHRAX NEXT TIME?

When this sobering thought was repeated in other avenues, the prime minister went on national television to exhort citizens to remain calm, but vigilant. Everything that could be done was being done, and he had every confidence that the instigators of these assaults against our democracy would be shortly brought to justice.

Behind the scenes, political pressure on ASIO and all the related intelligence and law enforcement bodies was intense. Privately, the prime minister had made it clear he believed the survival of his government was at stake, as members of the opposition, previously cowed by the ruling party's huge majority, had seized upon the situation, and were exploiting it to the full.

The Austral Trumpeter had the distinction of having been the bearer of bad but accurate news. A few days after the mailings, the editor contacted the Federal Police about a letter received at the paper's Sydney newsroom from someone claiming responsibility for the bio-terrorism scare.

Naturally, before contacting the authorities, *The Trump*—the shortened name by which the newspaper rapidly came to be called—splashed the text of the message over the front page of a special edition of the paper.

ANTHRAX TERRORISTS VOW: "THE REAL STUFF NEXT TIME"
PROMISE: "THOUSANDS WILL DIE"

When closely examined, the letter and envelope provided nothing useful. The envelope was similar to those used for the talcum powder mailing. A popular brand of laser printer had been used to print the letter on widely-distributed multi-use paper. The only fingerprints were those of the clerk in the newspaper's mailroom whose duty it was to open letters from the public and pass them on to the appropriate party for response. The moment he realized what it was, he'd placed the page in a transparent plastic sleeve—standard procedure at *The Trump* for threatening or suspicious letters.

The communication was short and to the point. After accurately listing post office locations where bundles of the mock-anthrax envelopes had been mailed, apparently to prove the communication was genuine, it ended with: *This first anthrax mailing is the promise of things to come. Next time it will be the real stuff. Weaponized anthrax. Thousands will die.*

The fact that this was the only newspaper receiving a purported letter from the terrorists was reason enough for ASIO to take a close look at the company. Jason Benton was the publisher and chief executive officer of *The Austral Trumpeter*, a new national newspaper modeled on *USA Today*.

Up to this point, the new boy on the block hadn't made much of a dent in the circulation figures of the competing national paper, *The Australian*, but the scoop *The Trump* achieved with the anthrax letter markedly improved its numbers, at least in the short term.

What was of particular interest in intelligence quarters was Jason Benton's silent partner, Emmaline Partlow, whose considerable financial assets backed the newspaper. An American, she enjoyed celebrity status as the founder and head of Supremity, which was registered as a church in the States, and was presently seeking the same tax-exempt basis in Australia.

Although Supremity categorized itself as a religion, one of its principal activities appeared to be enticing the famous to join the movement. Supremity claimed to be apolitical, but covertly the organization supported candidates of the extreme right, and there had been unsubstantiated rumors in the past that Emmaline Partlow herself had advocated violent means to achieve political ends.

Inconclusive reports from various sources suggested that Emmaline Partlow's organization had ties to extremist groups in the South Pacific region, including Australia. Vague accusations like this were common in intelligence work, and ASIO didn't give this information a great deal of weight until the death of a *Trump* junior reporter, Steven Ivers.

Ivers had contacted ASIO direct, claiming to have damning information related to Righteous Scourge and its connection to *The Austral Trumpeter*. He had hard evidence to back up his assertions, he said. As the newspaper's head office was in Sydney, arrangements were made for an operative to meet with Ivers at a designated safe house in one of the city's southern suburbs.

While riding his motorcycle to the appointment, Steven Ivers was run off the road by a battered pickup truck. Witnesses in passing vehicles saw two men leap from the truck and assumed they were rushing to help an accident victim. Instead, before fleeing the scene, accelerant was poured over both the wrecked motorcycle and the reporter's body. So fierce were the flames that the motorcycle's fuel tank exploded. Any material evidence Ivers might have been carrying was incinerated. Mercifully, an autopsy determined he'd been killed instantly by the initial impact.

Ivers had been one of several journalists working on a series exposing the tentacles of organized crime in the Asian community. His murder remained unsolved, but it was widely assumed that his death was somehow tied to his investigative reporting. *The Austral Trumpeter* arranged for a large memorial service, ran an obituary lauding Steven Ivers's journalistic courage and set up a fund in his name to support dependents of reporters killed in the line of duty.

The decision to insert an undercover agent into *The Trump's* newsroom was well into the planning stage when the next terrorist action instigated by Righteous Scourge began.

The sniper attacks started in a small town in northern Queensland. For a while it was thought to be a local problem, with some unbalanced individual taking random potshots at townspeople. Then, over the space of three days, six people were hit by sniper fire in Sydney, four in Melbourne and two in Hobart. Of the twelve victims, four were killed instantly, three, despite the best efforts, died soon afterwards and five were expected to live, although one of these victims had been shot through the spine and had been left a paraplegic.

Just like the 2002 sniper attacks in the Washington, D.C. area, these attacks seemed entirely arbitrary, with no discernable pattern as to time of day, selection of location or choice of victim. Male, female, young, old—it apparently made no difference. People were shot while going to the dentist, walking out of a supermarket, enjoying a day at the beach, filling a car at a service station, dropping the kids off at school . . .

The Righteous Scourge Web site, without comment, listed the victims by name and age. MORE TO COME was promised at the bottom of the column.

Two news outlets were contacted by the presumed snipers, who designated themselves by the name "Justice by the Gun." One news entity was *The Trump*, the other a television network. Both received the same rambling e-mail message, detailing the rifles and ammunition used and promising more deaths soon. The newspaper announced to its readers in a front page editorial that it had been contacted by the killers, but noted that law enforcement had begged *The Trump* not to print the message verbatim, and of course, the management would comply. However, the editor announced, as it was the duty of *The Austral Trumpeter* to keep its readers fully informed, page two carried a paraphrase of the contents.

The Trump's front page declared:

RIGHTEOUS SCOURGE SNIPER ATTACKS KILL, MAIM

PANIC SWEEPS NATION

In smaller letters it said:

PRIME MINISTER URGES CALM

He could urge all he liked, the population was not inclined
to remain unruffled by indiscriminate killings, where anyone
could become a victim without apparent rhyme or reason. An
ominous groundswell of negative public opinion seriously
alarmed the politicians in power, who began to demand answers
from the prime minister and his cabinet.

As it had gained the status of a sensational international
story, all Aussie media outlets were devoting considerable
resources to Righteous Scourge. Journalists poured in from
around the world. The governments of other countries quailed
at the thought that copycat Web sites could mean they might
soon be handling similar terrorism-for-hire civilian casualties.

The director-general of ASIO joined the heads of the
Australian Secret Intelligence Service, the Office of National
Assessments, the Defence Intelligence Organization and the
Federal Police in an urgent strategy meeting about the admin-
istration's ability to handle this escalating national emergency.

"Do everything necessary to make this go away," the prime
minister was reported to have said at the meeting. "You'll have
the funding, any personnel you need. Just do it, and do it fast!"

As one cog in this massive intelligence endeavor, I was about
to join *The Austral Trumpeter* in the role of consulting expert to a
team of reporters working on the Righteous Scourge story. And
in a delicious irony, my cover story was that I was a former officer of the DIO.

The Defence Intelligence Organisation was so secretive that

even we, in ASIO, were treated with disdain when seeking information. Irritating though this could be, in this instance it was an advantage. There was no way anyone would successfully penetrate DIO to check on my bona fides. At least I hoped that was true.

CHAPTER FOUR

I received a message that the three o'clock appointment had been pushed back to four. Absurdly nervous at the thought of seeing Roanna again, I made myself knock sharply on Keith Francis's office door, then opened it briskly when a voice called out to come in.

The room was empty, except for Cynthia, who was perched on the corner of Keith's desk. "Close the door and sit down," she said, not smiling.

Keith's office was just as idiosyncratic as Cynthia's, though his main decorating theme was related to his prowess with weapons. He had various plaques, cups and ribbons for his skill with handguns, rifles and shotguns. The walls were crowded with photographs of people holding various firearms while gazing—some cheerfully, some arrogantly—at the camera.

"What's cooking?" I asked.

"It seems Roanna Aylmer promises to be rather more useful than Keith at first supposed. He's kicked the whole thing upstairs. Right now she's with the top brass. Keith's there, too, as all this will have an impact on your assignment at *The Trump*."

Expressions usually chased each other across Cynthia's mobile face, but today she was as close to deadpan as I had ever seen her.

"You don't like her, do you?" I said, surprising myself with the question.

"No," said Cynthia.

"Why?"

Cynthia lifted her shoulders in a half shrug. "Because you do. Too much."

I stared at her, frankly amazed. She hadn't spoken in her usual brisk, ironic tone. "Cynthia?"

"Forget I said that."

"I don't know if I can."

She ran a hand through her spiky, dark red hair. "I'm not happy with this situation."

I felt I was in a conversation where I didn't know the rules. Was she talking in personal or professional terms? "What situation would that be?"

Cynthia slid off the edge of the desk and went over to look out the window. With her back to me, she said, "Roanna Aylmer has information, she claims, that implicates Jason Benton with Righteous Scourge. She says there's a good chance she's actually met the man behind the organization. That was enough to get her an interview with the director-general. She's there now."

"You think Roanna's lying?"

She swung around to look at me. "I believe she's a traitor, so yes, I think she's lying."

I shook my head. "No, Cynthia, she's not. I know Roanna. I'd stake my life on her loyalty to Australia."

Cynthia gave me an entirely unamused smile. "I'm afraid that's exactly what you'll be doing. I hope you're right about her, because she's already approached Benton with a business proposal involving the paper and her resort in some mutually advantageous scheme. It seems close to a sure thing you'll run into her at *The Trump.*"

I wasn't sure if that was welcome or unwelcome news. I always felt more secure if no one in the field knew I was an undercover agent. "So Roanna has to be briefed about my role as Ann Meadows."

Looking as if she'd bitten down on something sour, Cynthia said, "She already has the details." She paused, as if considering whether to say more, then went on, "I don't like it, Denise. It's too dangerous. The woman's an amateur. She could blow your cover, without even knowing she was doing it."

Cynthia had never unsettled me this way before. A wave of irritation made me snap, "Make up your mind, Cynthia. If Roanna's a traitor clever enough to escape prosecution when the rest of her family goes down, then she's no amateur."

"The alternative is hardly pleasant," said Cynthia harshly. "She's wormed her way into the middle of a covert assignment. She could use you to feed us disinformation."

Cynthia was right, of course. And because I'd been trained, where national security was concerned, to trust no one, I had to admit to myself the possibility Roanna's approach to ASIO was part of a scheme to provide us with a stream of bogus intelligence.

"It's a remote likelihood," I said, "but I don't believe it."

We both looked around as the door opened.

"Denise," said Roanna. She hadn't changed. She was exactly

the same magnetically attractive woman—slim, dark-haired and with an arrogant set to her mouth.

"Hi," I said, carefully noncommittal.

Keith Francis grinned wolfishly as he ushered her into the room. He was obviously pleased to have such a coup to bring to the director-general. "Take a seat, Roanna, and tell Denise the interesting things you've been saying about Jason Benton and Emmaline Partlow."

"They're an item?" I asked flippantly.

"They were," said Roanna, "when they visited the resort four years ago. Very much so."

Keith, who'd taken the seat behind his desk, leaned back in his chair with a laugh. "Bit of an age difference, eh? She'd have ten years on him, wouldn't you say?"

No one bothered to respond to his remark. At last he cleared his throat and filled the silence with, "Benton visited the Aylmer Resort on several occasions that particular year, but only once—his final visit—was he accompanied by the Partlow woman."

"It was business as well as pleasure," said Roanna. "Emmaline was providing a great deal of money to launch his newspaper."

Keith smiled at Roanna in a mildly ingratiating way. "And on the pleasure side, I believe your Aylmer Resort is very luxurious and very beautiful."

Perhaps he was angling for an invitation to the island. If so, he was disappointed, because Roanna merely said, "Thank you."

I'd been at the resort undercover three years ago, so Benton's visits had occurred prior to my time there. Close to an earthly paradise, Aylmer Resort, which Roanna was now running solo, was situated on an island near the Great Barrier Reef. Gorgeous though the island was, the ugliness of the Aylmer family's betrayal of Australia had poisoned it for me. I'd never been back, even though Roanna had asked me several times to return. I'd always used the excuse that anyone who'd been working on the island when I'd been playing the role of bartender might recognize me.

It unnerved me a little to see that Cynthia was sitting bolt upright in her chair, both feet on the floor. This posture was so uncharacteristic that when she glanced my way, I raised my eyebrows in an unspoken question. She ignored me, saying acidly to Roanna, "Apparently, Benton found George and Moreen Aylmer to be his political soul mates."

Roanna's expression didn't change at the mention of her parents, now serving life sentences in separate federal prisons. "Jason was in the initial planning stages for *The Austral Trumpeter*," she said. "He'd bring a different executive with him each time he visited us. We put him and his guest in separate luxury cabanas in our family compound. My mother admired Jason and encouraged me to be friendly with him, pointing out that she could see many positives in having a future press baron on our side."

Moreen Aylmer had been the matriarch of the family business, which had two aspects: the very profitable luxury tropical resort and the criminal operation of an even more profitable espionage undertaking. She was a lethal creature, her patrician elegance disguising her skills at pulling strings and manipulating powerful people to do her will. I'd never forgotten her stone-cold face, as she'd sent me to what she believed would be my certain death.

"Have you seen your mother lately?" I asked.

Roanna gave me a faint, cynical smile. "You know I have, since every meeting is monitored. I visit my parents and my brother Harry on a regular basis."

Up until now, whether or not Roanna visited her incarcerated family was not on the list of items ASIO considered I needed to know. And when Roanna and I had been involved romantically, I'd never brought the subject up. How could I? After all, I'd been the one most responsible for bringing the family down. I wondered, since Roanna had given evidence against the three, what sort of reception she got when she saw them.

"Regular basis?" said Cynthia. "Every six months, isn't it? Not what I'd call attentive."

Roanna's face hardened. "I don't condone what my parents and Harry did, but I consider it my duty to see them at least twice a year."

Cynthia, who was looking grimly intent, managed an icy smile. "Your duty? Is that why you raised the matter of Righteous Scourge with your mother last week?"

"I'm aware every word is recorded," Roanna said. "No doubt you've seen transcripts of our conversation, so you know exactly what I asked her and how my mother replied."

Clearly, Cynthia was conversant with what had been said. "When you brought up the subject, your mother said she and your father had talked with Benton about many things, and she couldn't remember if he'd ever mentioned such a group."

"My mother is not telling the truth. While Jason was at the resort, I heard Righteous Scourge mentioned quite often—I remember because I thought it an almost laughably pretentious name—but I don't recall the context, only that Jason had some strong views on the subject. And one time, this man came over from the mainland for the day to see Jason and my parents. With the benefit of hindsight, I'm almost sure he had something to do with Righteous Scourge, because that is one time I definitely remember the subject came up that morning at breakfast, and when the guy arrived, my parents and Jason disappeared for hours into the conference room."

"Unfortunately," said Keith, "Roanna doesn't recall this individual's name—if she ever knew it. And she only has the vaguest memory of what he looked like."

Cynthia gave a contemptuous snort. "Such convenient amnesia."

Roanna eyed her coolly, then said, "Politics bores me. I grew up listening to arguments about government failings and radical movements. Any mention of Righteous Scourge, or anyone who might be associated with it, was just more of the same. Frankly, I didn't pay much attention."

Affronted, Keith said, "But you told the director-general—"

"I know what I told the director-general, and it was true. Jason frequently discussed terrorist organizations—the Tamil Tigers, al-Qaida, the Basque Separatists—and the inadequate responses various governments made in the face of terror campaigns. I remember him mentioning Righteous Scourge as a developing terrorist movement."

Cynthia gave a sharp laugh. "All this discussion of terrorism, and you never suspected your family was up to their necks in espionage? Not surprisingly, I find that almost impossible to believe."

Roanna shrugged. "My parents and my two brothers held radical positions politically. I didn't share those views. I had no reason to suppose they were actively involved in anything that would harm my country."

Cynthia's skeptical expression impelled Roanna to add, "Look, I wasn't charged with anything. There's no evidence against me. Therefore it follows there's no point in you hounding me this way."

Keith put up his hands in a placating manner. I thought he might put his foot in his mouth, and say something like: "Now let's be proper ladies here, please!" but he was more circumspect.

30

"We're offering Moreen Aylmer privileges for information," he said. "So far she hasn't bitten. Nor has her husband George shown any interest in our quite generous offers to make life in prison more comfortable for him. Fortunately there's Harry, Roanna's brother. He seems more amenable."

"Harry will string you along," Roanna said, a hint of derision in her voice. "I doubt my brother knows anything of use, but he'll imply he does, just to see what advantages he can wring out of you."

"Maybe *you're* the one stringing *us* along," snapped Cynthia, her hostility plain. "And I'm asking myself, what's in it for you?"

Roanna glared back at her. "Nothing's in it for me, personally. Absolutely nothing."

The phone on Keith's desk rang. He clicked his tongue in irritation. "I told them, no calls. Doesn't anybody follow instructions anymore?" He snatched up the receiver. "Yes?"

I watched his expression change. He asked a few questions, then hung up. "Oh, Christ," he said. "It's bad enough when these bloody snipers are killing ordinary run-of-the-mill citizens—now they've really gone too far."

"A public figure?" I said.

"You could say that. The number-one ranked tennis star . . . the Yank . . . what's his name . . . ?"

"Noah Craddock?" said Cynthia.

"That's the guy. He's playing in a tournament in Brisbane. Big crowds, and the media are there in force, of course. Craddock's just about to serve out the final set when someone puts a bullet right in the center of his forehead. He pitches over, dead, at the baseline. No suspects. No one sees anything suspicious before or after the shot."

"Noah Craddock?" said Roanna, looking totally shocked. "My God, I've met him. He was a guest on the island."

There was a moment of silence while everyone absorbed the

news. Noah Craddock had had a meteoric rise in the world of tennis. He was unfailingly gracious, whether winning or losing, photogenic and had recently married one of the ubiquitous Russian tennis players with a multi-syllabic name.

"Media firestorm," Cynthia remarked.

Keith sighed. "Worse. International incident. The CIA'll be on us like a ton of bricks."

CHAPTER FIVE

As an ASIO agent, I had an excellent background in terrorism and the responses required to combat it. What I required now was to get into the skin of the fictional Ann Meadows and present her as a real, rounded personality with an expertise in urban terrorism.

Such experts were in high demand because the various media outlets were scrambling to come up with new angles on the attacks, particularly for the sniper story. The executive editor of *The Austral Trumpeter* was an American woman, Paula Valentine, and like all her media peers, she actively cultivated contacts in the intelligence community.

When Paula Valentine put out feelers for a suitable terrorism specialist to advise the paper, ASIO made sure the name of Ann Meadows was given to her from an impeccable source deep in DIO. The Defence Intelligence Organisation had a much lower profile than ASIO—in essence, as far as the general public was concerned, it had no profile at all—so she was forced to take her contact's word that Ann Meadows had recently taken early retirement from DIO and would be an excellent recruit to the newspaper's team.

Thus vouched for, I'd had no problem with a face-to-face interview, which had taken place at the beginning of the week. Paula Valentine was a slight woman, looking much younger than her age, with waist-length black hair and a serene manner, which entirely contradicted the ruthless reputation attributed to her in my briefing papers.

With brave-widow demeanor, I'd told her how I'd retired from DIO to nurse my ailing husband, who had since died. As a precaution, ASIO had provided this fictional husband of mine with both birth and death certificates, plus a medical history, but little else. This would not be a red flag to any investigator, as my spouse had also worked for DIO, and so public records were, of necessity, very limited.

Now I was on my way to my final training session with Dr. Estelle Decker, a psychiatrist who was a consultant to ASIO. She was an acknowledged international authority on terrorism in all its manifestations. Estelle had previously coached me for an earlier undercover mission where I had to play a therapist, so I knew her to be an excellent if rather wry teacher. Normally I would have had to travel to Sydney to meet with her, but she had come to Canberra for a series of lectures at the university and had fitted my sessions into her schedule.

Anyone introduced to Dr. Estelle Decker for the first time would almost invariably misjudge her. She looked like an untidy, good-intentioned grandmother. Well-upholstered, she always wore loose, comfortable clothes that appeared to have been thrown on without much thought for whether items matched each other.

People taken in by her mild, scatterbrained appearance soon found the error of their ways. She was prodigiously intelligent, and had no time for the indecisive, the ineffectual or the spineless. She'd shocked quite a few with her bawdy humor.

I liked her very much.

As soon as she opened the door of her suite—she always insisted on staying at the best hotels—Estelle waved me over to a chair near the window and, ignoring social pleasantries, said, "Well, Denise, the shit's hit the fan with the Craddock murder. You can knock off the odd politician, and nobody cares all that much, but a sports star? That's a different matter."

The media firestorm Cynthia had predicted was already underway. It was still early morning in the States, and people would be waking up to learn one of their most admired athletic heroes had been murdered in far-off Australia. Here, of course, it was the lead story on the evening news.

Driving over to the hotel, I'd listened to the Queensland minister for tourism saying how deeply concerned she was that this dreadful tragedy might negatively impact the number of American tourists entering Australia. She was followed by a sports analyst, who called it "a devastating sporting tragedy," and then lamented that professional sportsmen and women would undoubtedly be thinking twice before competing in our country. Just as I reached the hotel, an announcement was made that the prime minister would address the nation at eight o'clock.

"The PM's making a statement at eight," I said to Estelle.

She sniffed. "Out of his depth. A poor, sniveling creature. Irresolute. Indecisive." She fixed me with a penetrating look. "Ann Meadows, whom you'll soon be—how did she vote? For the prime minister?"

This was a good question. I had to assume my new identity so completely that I could answer without hesitation. "Ann did vote for his party, and therefore for his leadership, but it was because she sees herself as a conservative, not because she favored him. As a prime minister, he's too wishy-washy for her."

"Describe her character to me, Denise."

"Somewhat of a bore, actually. Uptight. Pedantic. A person inclined to launch into lectures in her area of expertise, perhaps to impress people."

Dr. Estelle frowned. "Perhaps? You should *know* her motivations."

"She's not aware of why she does it," I said quickly, grinning. "Our Ann is a trifle low on self-knowledge."

"And sexually? What's her sex life like?"

"She doesn't have any at the moment. Ann's a widow, and still stricken with grief in a well-mannered fashion, so she's not dating. Besides, casual sex is out, anyway. She believes in marriage."

"So she's heterosexual?"

"Well, of course," I said primly, just as Ann Meadows would. "Anything else would be unnatural."

"Masturbation?"

"Heavens, no!" I exclaimed. "Hairy palms? Deafness? That's not for her."

Estelle laughed, then said, "For our last session, let's role play, shall we? I'll be someone you meet in the newsroom of *The Austral Trumpeter.*" She thought for a moment. "I'm a junior reporter, with ambitions to make the big time."

She could have had a career as an actor, for in an instant her body language and facial expressions belonged to another person—someone younger, less-accomplished, but with an intense curiosity, an admirable trait in a reporter.

"Hi," she said, "I'm Sherry Smith. And you are?"

I hid a smile, and said solemnly, "Ann Meadows. Nice to meet you, Sherry."

"Oh! I've heard of you. You must be the expert on urban terrorism."

"That's what they tell me."

The fictional Sherry Smith was looking at me with the keenest interest. "I wonder if I could pick your brains, Ann? I've got this story coming up, and I need a general background in terrorism. Since it's your area . . ."

"Sure. What do you want to know?"

"Well . . . everything. Like why people become terrorists. I mean, they have to be psychopathic don't they? That, or really, really evil?"

"Terrorism is a highly complex subject, not a simple phenomenon that can be combated with easy solutions," I began in a pompous tone. Estelle/Sherry looked suitably entranced.

I went on, "As for the terrorists themselves, there's a tendency to try to explain extreme violence against innocent victims by describing the perpetrators as psychologically abnormal, as if no ordinary, sane person could possibly commit such wicked, inhuman acts."

I paused for a self-deprecating half smile. "Indeed, you might not believe this, Sherry, but when experts, such as myself, explore the motivations of specific terrorists, we run the chance of being thought of as somehow sympathetic to them, because we seek to understand why they did what they did."

Sherry was shaking her head. "But how can they be sane? They do such *awful* things."

I hopped back on my soapbox. "The sheer callousness of terrorist attacks, typically with multiple casualties, often including children, provokes in people deep feelings of rage, horror and a burning desire for revenge."

"I feel vengeful," announced Sherry, stoutly militant.

"Then, Sherry, you can clearly see how objective analysis goes out the door. Strong emotions overcome cool analysis.

Politicians and the public demonize the perpetrators, assuming them to be virulent fanatics against whom the most extreme measures must be used. The usual rules of law are suspended, and anyone suspected of being a terrorist can expect to lose most, if not all, the rights most citizens enjoy."

Hell, droning on like this, I was boring myself.

Sherry, however, maintained a flattering expression of lively interest. "So terrorists aren't insane or unbalanced?" she inquired.

"They're rarely crazy, although it is a comfort to many people to believe they are. Otherwise, how could anyone do what the terrorist has done? What sane person can kill innocent men, women and children? How can someone normal be prepared to sacrifice his or her own life in the process of murdering and maiming other humans?"

Indignation flooded Sherry's face. "I'm sure no one normal *could* do these dreadful things."

"The truth, Sherry, is very disturbing," I said, super-solemnly. "I've read widely in this area, and studied material from many in-depth interviews of perpetrators who've committed almost unimaginable acts of violence. From the psychiatric viewpoint, you may be shocked to learn the majority of terrorists are *not* abnormal. They don't share the psychological traits of the majority of very violent criminals, who can usefully be categorized as psychotics, neurotics, fanatics or sociopaths."

I had to smile at myself. "Got a bit carried away there, Sherry," I said.

"You're not telling me they're just ordinary people?" Sherry sounded scandalized.

"Actually, I am telling you that. With few exceptions, they *are* ordinary. Most terrorists experience the normal emotions of anxiety and fear whilst carrying out their most lethal attacks on other people. They are not simple killing machines, so fanatical that ordinary feelings are impossible for them. What they are, however, is totally and utterly convinced that what they do is right."

I knew what I was saying was backed with evidence from many psychological assessments and analysis of debriefings of captured terrorists, but it was hard, even for me, to accept that almost anyone, given the right environment and situation, was capable of such dreadful crimes.

I became aware that Estelle/Sherry was giving me a challenging look. "Okay," she said, "I want you to explain to me exactly how someone gets to be a terrorist, if, like you say, they're so normal."

"Why does someone become what I may categorize as a classic terrorist?" Pause for reflection. "Generally it's a gradual process of socialization, followed by some overwhelming event of excessive violence by forces of the establishment, such as law enforcement or the military."

"In Australia?" said Sherry, deeply incredulous. "I mean, the cops can be a bit rough at times . . . but enough to turn someone into a terrorist?"

"There will always be minority groups who feel disaffected and unfairly treated," I intoned. "Individuals who identify with such a group—based on religious, racial, cultural differences to the larger society—share a deep sense of injustice and alienation."

I raised an admonishing finger. "And remember, Sherry, their grievance may be absolutely genuine. When people close to them—friends, colleagues, family members—are abused, maimed or killed, this extreme physical violence from the all-powerful authorities tips potential terrorists over into a full embrace of ferocious aggression as a personal, political act. It seems to them this is the only way their overwhelming anger and desire for vengeance can be expressed."

"You sound sorry for them, Ann." Plainly Sherry did not approve.

"Not at all! Before I sound too sympathetic, let me point out I accept totally that terrorist organizations are pitiless and chillingly brutal. They deliberately fan the fires of profound emotions such as alienation and sense of injustice, in order to inoculate members against the normal responses of empathy and sorrow at human carnage."

Estelle leaned back grinning. She gave me a slow handclap. "My work here is done. Ann Meadows is the most stultifyingly boring individual I've come across for a long time. Congratulations."

"I've nailed her, you think?"

"You have."

Before I left, we revised details specific to urban terrorism. I had exhaustive reports of the attacks so far, so I had studied analyses of the state of mind and motivations for each of the three amateur terrorists who'd been arrested. For the most recent anthrax mailings and the sniper killings, I'd examined American information, particularly the random sniper spree committed by John Allen Muhammad and the much younger Lee Boyd Malvo.

To celebrate the end of my training, Estelle called room service for a bottle of champagne. While we waited for it to be delivered, she said to me, "What do you think of Cynthia's plans. Quite a surprise, wasn't it?"

"Plans about what?"

She raised her eyebrows. "Cynthia hasn't told you?"

"Obviously not."

Looking uncomfortable, Estelle said, "I hadn't realized . . . I've put myself in an awkward position. I don't know—"

"Oh, go on," I said. "Tell me. If you don't, I'll march right over and ask Cynthia anyway."

"Cynthia's taking early retirement."

My jaw actually dropped. Recovering, I said, "Cynthia? Retirement? I don't believe it. What will she do with herself?"

Estelle was looking at me speculatively. "It's odd, Denise, but the way Cynthia speaks of you, I'd assumed you were close friends."

"We have a close professional relationship. Not a personal one."

"So you're not aware of her standing in the world of art?"

If these revelations kept coming, I'd be in a perpetual state of astonishment. "Enlighten me."

"She's quite a notable sculptor. Uses the name Willow Trent."

I frowned. Somehow the name touched a faint memory. "There was something about a sculpture in a courtyard at National University?"

"That's right. Bit of a brouhaha. It was highly abstract, but some uptight individuals claimed it was obscene."

"Was it?"

Estelle laughed immoderately. "Absolutely."

As soon as I got home, I called Cynthia. The number was an ASIO one, and automatically rerouted to her, wherever she might be.

The moment she answered, I said, "When were you going to tell me?"

"Denise?"

"Estelle Decker spilled the beans."

"Oh."

Suddenly I was furious. "Oh? Is that all you can say?"

Silence. I went on, "I mean, this is just great. Terrific. I'll be in the middle of an assignment, and my contact will disappear. Is that what's going to happen? Here one day, gone the next?"

"Of course not. I'm not going anywhere until after this job is completed, however long it takes."

Abruptly, my anger dissipated. Now I was upset. "Why didn't you tell me you were leaving ASIO? We've worked together for so long. I thought we were friends."

"Denise, we *are* friends. Perhaps that's why I've delayed saying anything. I knew it would be . . . hard."

Ridiculously, I felt my eyes sting with tears. "I have to leave early tomorrow. Sorry, I've got to go."

"Denise—"

I hung up, turned on the television for background noise, then hunted around and found a bottle of bourbon. I rarely drank hard liquor, but tonight was going to be an exception. The hasty glass of champagne I'd had with Estelle hadn't even given me a buzz—now I'd get down to serious drinking.

That was my intention, but one glass of bourbon, even drowned in Coca-Cola, was all I could manage. I sipped it like medicine, spreading it out over half an hour, in the vain hope that my taste buds would become accustomed to the stuff. There had to be some alternative to bourbon. Further investigation revealed an unopened bottle of sweet sherry—yuck— and a half bottle of gin. I was morosely considering my options when the front doorbell rang.

I had a full security system, but I didn't really need to look at the video screen to know that it was Cynthia. She'd never visited my little house before, but of course she knew everything about me, including basic information like where I lived when I wasn't on assignment.

Flinging open the door, I said, "Come in. I can offer you bourbon, sweet sherry or gin. Or coffee."

"Coffee, please."

One thing I did know about Cynthia was that she was a vegetarian. I wondered if that meant she'd only drink decaffeinated. "I've only got straight coffee."

"Straight coffee?" she said with the beginnings of a smile. "What if I prefer gay?"

I let that pass. "I'll be a few moments." I glanced around my bland living room. I wasn't home often enough to imprint it with much personality. I couldn't even have houseplants because they'd die from neglect. "Make yourself comfortable."

"I'd rather come to the kitchen, with you."

Loose-limbed, she perched on a tall kitchen stool and watched me as I ground the coffee beans. The roar of the grinder precluded conversation. What had she meant by *gay*? Was that a code of some kind? A joke?

"You're Willow Trent," I said when the noise ceased.

"Yes."

"Are those sculptures in your office your work?"

"Do you like them?" she inquired.

"No."

"Then they're not my work."

I sat down on a stool opposite her. "Cynthia, why are you here?"

"To apologize."

"For not telling me you are leaving ASIO?"

"To apologize for a lot of things, but mainly for not being honest with you."

Not knowing what to say, I didn't speak. Cynthia made a face at me. "You're not going to make this easy, are you?"

"What is it that I'm not making easy?"

With angular grace, she slid off the stool and came over to me. "This," she said, and kissed me, very gently, on the lips.

CHAPTER SIX

Tomorrow I would begin my first full day of employment with *The Austral Trumpeter*. The newspaper was situated in the inner city suburb of Darlington, so ASIO had rented a small furnished flat in Ann Meadows's name in Alexandria, an adjacent suburb. Once a working class area, now, like so much of inner Sydney, Alexandria was becoming gentrified.

I got up before dawn and packed the clothes that had been selected as typical of the sort Ann Meadows would wear—sensible, conservative garments in muted colors. Similarly, Ann's underwear was mundane—she favored natural fibers when possible and wore cotton pajamas. Not, of course, that I was necessarily expecting such intimate clothing to be exposed to view, but I had to be Ann Meadows completely.

I left Canberra to drive the three hundred kilometers to

Sydney when it was still very early. This afternoon I was to visit the newsroom to meet the team assembled to concentrate on Righteous Scourge. For the last few days I'd been reading past editions of the paper to familiarize myself with the work of reporters who'd soon be my colleagues. ASIO researchers had compiled a file on each person I was expected to meet. Photographs were included, plus a general overview of career and background.

My vehicle was an anonymous sedan registered and insured in the name of Ann Meadows. It wasn't an exhilarating machine, but it zipped along quite satisfactorily. I usually enjoyed this drive, beginning with the loop of the Federal Highway around Lake George, a body of water with the unnerving quality of rising and falling—sometimes coming close to draining away—without any apparent reason. Then I'd join the Hume Highway, traveling northeast on a long diagonal until I reached Sydney on the coast.

This morning, however, my chaotic thoughts blinded me to the beautiful country I was driving through. That one kiss last night had had the most unexpected effect on me. I'd always found Cynthia intriguing, but unattainable, so had never seriously considered her as lover material. Now futures I'd never visualized opened like flowers before me.

She hadn't stayed for coffee. I'd seen her out somewhat in a daze, with what she'd just said to me in the kitchen running in a half-exciting, half-alarming loop in my head.

After that jolting, gentle kiss, she'd stepped back. I imagine I looked as startled as I felt. She put out a hand and touched my cheek. "Denise, I'm not saying there is, or will be, anything between us, but I want you to know that at least on my side, there's a possibility, now that I'm leaving ASIO."

She'd given me her charming, crooked smile. "From the first

time we met, I felt something, but that tug of attraction was relatively easy to disregard. Recently it's become much harder to ignore—almost impossible, actually."

I'd said, "You know everything about me. I don't know anything about you. About your personal life."

"Any question you ask, I'll answer. But only after this assignment is completed." She'd grimaced. "Forgive me. It's a distraction you don't need, me coming here tonight. I'm sorry."

"It's okay," I'd said, my mind already teeming with questions: What past relationships had she had? Exclusively with women? Or was she bisexual? Had she ever been married? How had she become a sculptor? And what was the real reason she was leaving ASIO?

At the door, I'd said formally, "Goodnight, Courtney. I'll be speaking with you soon."

"Goodnight, Ann Meadows. I look forward to hearing your voice."

Sleep hadn't come easily last night, and I yawned as I drove. I stopped at Goulburn for breakfast and a substantial caffeine fix. While I ate, I mentally reviewed *The Trump's* editorial chain of command. At the top, of course, was the publisher and chief executive officer, Jason Benton. Directly under him was Paula Valentine, the executive editor, who I'd already met at my Ann Meadows job interview.

The organization then split into two divisions—news and opinion. Warwick Wallace was the managing editor—news. Oliver Yorkin was managing editor—opinion. Each had deputy managing editors under them. Of particular interest to me was Stella Rohm, who reported to Warwick Wallace, because she was the one directly in charge of the Righteous Scourge team.

On the road again, I turned my thoughts to my romantic life—or lack of it. Until Cynthia's astonishing declaration last night, in the last few years there'd only been two women I'd held dear to my heart, and I'd met both while on undercover assignments.

The first had been Roanna Aylmer, the second, Siobhan Hurdstone. In both cases geographic obstacles had caused difficulties. Roanna and I had drifted apart, in some measure because she managed the family resort off the Queensland coast, and I was located wherever my next assignment took me. In Siobhan's case, her billionaire father had established the Hurdstone Peace Foundation, and Siobhan would devote months, sometimes years, on projects around the globe.

And now I could add Cynthia to this very short romantic list. Or perhaps not. What did I really know of her, after all? She was excellent at her job, she had a delightful, dry sense of humor but nothing else except, like me, ASIO's rigorous standards had judged her acceptable to serve her country. Oh, and she was Willow Trent, sculptor.

Last night, before going to bed, I'd sat at my computer and Googled the name Willow Trent. In art circles she was clearly famous, but also controversial. I frowned over photographs of various Willow Trent sculptures, searching for a word to describe them. *Strange* came to mind. Could one love the artist, but not her work?

I shook my head in exasperation. There was no point in letting my thoughts run on like this. It wasn't as though there was more between us than a light kiss in my kitchen. Still, it made my pulse jump to recall the unmistakable cadences of Cynthia's unique voice saying, "Recently it's become harder to ignore—impossible, actually."

Traffic was unexpectedly heavy long before I reached the edges of Sydney proper, so I had to rush to make my appointment at *The Trump*. I stopped by my flat to drop off my suitcases and change from jeans into something more suitable for Ann Meadows to wear. The team setting up my accommodation had stocked the wardrobe with additional clothes. I chose a conservative navy blue suit with a pale blue silk blouse. My shoes had sensible heels, not too high. For jewelry I put on tasteful pearl earrings and a delicate gold watch.

Before I left, I checked that everything was secure. The ground floor flat had a private entrance, so that other tenants would not see me coming and going. Anyone approaching the front door would be caught by a surveillance camera and shown on a small security monitor in the living room. All windows had double locks and curtains of opaque material. The phone had been set up so that any calls I made would be close to impossible to intercept. And, although I hoped I'd never need it, a concealed drawer in the kitchen held a fully-loaded Glock.

On my way out, I picked up the ultra-thin powder blue briefcase that had been left just inside the front door for me. The briefcase, discreetly embossed with Ann's initials, held, I knew, extracts of various articles pertaining to my supposed field of expertise. Plus an expensive gold fountain pen—Ann Meadows was the fountain pen type—a business diary full of various fictitious appointments—Ann Meadows was not keen on electronic organizers—and a phone—Ann Meadows *did* believe in mobile phones.

I galloped out to my car and set out in the direction of the newspaper's offices. Having closely studied street maps of all the surrounding areas, I found my destination without trouble. In any case, the building would be hard to miss. It had alternating turquoise and white floors, and looming atop it was a gigantic, stylized golden figure blowing a gigantic gold trumpet. THE AUSTRAL TRUMPETER appeared in fat gold letters over the trumpeter's head.

I checked my watch as I drew up in one of the visitor's bays of the underground parking structure. Ann Meadows would never be late. A little early would be best, but I didn't have that option. I'd have to hurry to make it exactly on time.

Cynthia reminded me during our last training session that the junior reporter, Steven Ivers, had met his death while driving to meet ASIO officers with what he'd claimed was evidence that would link the newspaper with Righteous Scourge. "It's possible someone there is directly responsible for his death. Never forget that any one of the people you will be dealing with on a daily basis could be a murderer."

Violence seemed a foreign concept in these palatial offices. Paula Valentine herself was waiting for me at the sleek reception desk. I knew her to be almost fifty—she looked to be in her late thirties. She'd been married three times, divorced twice, so she still had her third husband, a self-styled entrepreneur in his thirties, who had yet to achieve conspicuous success at anything, although ASIO's file on Paula Valentine included the notation that he was considering a career in politics.

"Ann! So nice to see you again." At our first meeting she'd asked me to call her by her first name, so I murmured, "Paula," diffidently.

Her very long, dark hair swung around her as she did a graceful turn. "I'll take you directly to Stella's office. She's waiting to meet you with the keenest anticipation."

"How nice," I said.

Entirely disregarding my vacuous comment, Paula Valentine called out, "Brad? Do you have a moment?"

Brad, who'd been passing by, immediately turned and headed our way. He was extremely handsome. Tall, well-built and with lots of curly, dark hair, I reckoned he was one of those very good-looking people who automatically trade on their looks.

He flashed us both a quick, white smile. I imagined it would be instantly extinguished if he found out I knew he'd recently had liposuction for love handles.

"Hello there. You must be Ann," he said to me, taking my hand. Looking deep into my eyes, he breathed, "I'm delighted that we'll be working together."

"Meet Brad Thomson," said Paula Valentine. "He's on the Righteous team. One of our top reporters."

"How do you do?" I said.

He laughed roguishly. "If you must know, I do very well." Still gripping my hand, he gave me a meaningful look. "And with you here, I expect to do even better."

I glanced at Paula V. She didn't appear offended by her employee's excessively familiar manner to a stranger. Ann Meadows, however, would not be as sanguine. I frowned, extracted my fingers from his grip, and looked pointedly at Paula V. "You said Ms. Rohm is waiting to meet me?"

Brad interposed before she could speak. "Paula, I'll take Ann along. Save you some time. A busy executive like you must have a million things on your plate."

Groan. I would have slapped him down, if I'd been her, but she merely nodded to us both, did her hair swing thing again, and set off with graceful strides in the opposite direction.

"This is kind of you, Mr. Thomson."

"*Brad*, please. We're all on first name terms here."

He moved to take my elbow, but I did a neat sidestep to avoid him. "I've read some of your work, Brad. I must say I particularly admired your in-depth piece about Noah Craddock, the tennis player killed by the sniper. It was excellent."

And it was. Brad Thomson might be Mr. All-Too-Charming in person, but in print he was an artist.

I thought he might be gratified by my compliment, but he gave no sign he'd even heard me. Perhaps he was accustomed to praise and took it as his due. "Stella's office is along this way," he said. "What do you think of her name?"

"I beg your pardon?"

"Stella. Like in *A Streetcar Named Desire*." He halted, threw back his head and bellowed, "Stella!" then looked at me expectantly.

"Marlon Brando," I said.

He gave me a thumbs-up, yelled "Stella!" again, then, with a little-boy, mischievous smile, said in his normal voice, "Drives Stella mad."

"I can see how it would."

His smile disappeared at my cool tone. "It's just a bit of fun, Ann. Tension-relieving."

"Really? Aren't you increasing Stella Rohm's tension by yelling her name in a Brando impersonation?"

He looked to see if there was any sign of humor on my face. There wasn't. But I saw a hint of uncertainty in his manner and suddenly realized he wasn't nearly as sure of himself as he wanted me—and no doubt everyone else—to think.

Stella Rohm was tailored, forceful and brisk. She dismissed him with, "Thanks, Brad. If you get the others together in the conference room, Ann and I will meet you there in fifteen minutes."

After he'd left, she came over to shake hands with me.

"I'm pleased to meet you, Ms. Rohm," I said, all cool efficiency.

"First names," she said. "It's the rule here at *The Trump*. From the publisher right down the line."

Stella had very short blond hair, a tanned, intense face and was heading for zero body fat. I knew from her file she was at the gym most days, and on the weekend ran with a cross-country club. This was one seriously fit individual.

She indicated I should sit, and I did so, neatly arranging my legs and feet as a true lady would. Stella remained standing. She picked up a folder from her desk, flipped over a few pages, and said, "So, Ann, you were with DIO for several years. That must have been very interesting."

"I'm sorry, I can't discuss anything to do with the Defence Intelligence Organisation," I said stuffily. "I'm constrained by law."

"Paula believes your standing as an expert in the area of urban terrorism will enable my team to access valuable background information." Her tone suggested she had deep reservations about this being the case.

My manner conveying slighted dignity, I said, "You have doubts about my worth? Perhaps you fail to see that it lies in whom I know, not merely what I know."

"Indeed? Explain."

"In the course of your investigative journalism, you will come across many pieces of information, some of it, when put in context, vital to uncovering the perpetrators of these outrageous attacks." I smiled inwardly. I sounded incredibly pompous.

In the same irritating tone, I continued, "The problem will be, I venture to say, to determine what information is gold and what is dross. My friends and former colleagues in the intelligence community can provide the necessary context. It will be, I am hopeful, a mutually beneficial relationship that will ultimately bring these terrorists to justice."

Stella didn't roll her eyes, but I could tell she was fighting the impulse. If we'd been featured in a comic strip, a bubble over her head would sum up her opinion of me in one short phrase: self-important bitch.

Ann Meadows was just the sort of person I couldn't stand either, but I had to admit it was fun playing her.

I checked my watch. "I believe you said to Brad you'd introduce me to the team in a quarter of an hour. Surely the time will be up any moment now. I never like to keep people waiting."

Stella glared at me. She took a breath to speak, but I was never to know what she was about to say as, unannounced, a young woman shot into the room, carrying a purple gym bag. "Oh, sorry, Stella," she blurted out in one of those very nasal American accents, "I didn't realize you had someone here."

I recognized her immediately—Emmaline Partlow's personal assistant. She was carrying a little weight, which showed because she wasn't very tall. She wore her brown hair long and pulled back with a tortoiseshell clip.

Holding out my hand, I said, "Ann Meadows. I'm joining *The Trump* as an urban terrorism expert." I cast a look over to Stella. "I've got it right, haven't I? People here do call *The Austral Trumpeter* by the diminutive, *The Trump*?"

Stella nodded without much enthusiasm.

"Lorna Gosling," the young woman said, dropping her gym bag and wringing my fingers hard.

I resisted wringing them right back, instead letting a look of pain cross my face. "You have quite a grip, Lorna."

"Oh, *sorry*! It's the rubber balls. You squeeze them to strengthen your hands."

Politely incredulous, I said, "Really? I had no idea."

"I'm getting fit with Stella's help," she confided. "It's just so wonderful to exercise with a friend. I've only been doing it a few weeks, but already I've lost *pounds*."

Harps sounded. I looked around for a possible angelic appearance, but Lorna was busy diving into her purple gym bag. "My cell phone, I'm afraid!" Anxiety crossed her face. "It's Emmaline! Excuse me, I must take this."

She listened, then looked at me wide-eyed. "Why yes, she is here . . . Of course, I'll tell her."

Stella made a mildly derisive sound. "I'd say you're summoned for an audience with Emmaline Partlow," she said to me.

I wrinkled my brow. "Why would Emmaline Partlow want to see me?"

Lorna finished the call. "Emmaline's invited you to dinner," she said, not hiding her astonishment. "Tonight. Eight. I'm to give you the directions."

"Good luck," said Stella. "She's like a human lie detector. Try to bullshit her, she'll know, right away."

CHAPTER SEVEN

Brad Thomson had everyone assembled when Stella and I entered the sumptuous conference room, which had paneled walls, thick, thick cream carpet and a huge, handcrafted rosewood table surrounded by matching chairs. It was obvious Jason Benton had spared no expense to make the head office of *The Trump* extravagantly luxurious, no doubt using Emmaline Partlow's money to achieve this opulence. I wondered what she got out of this partnership. Establishing a newspaper was a costly enterprise, and the analysis of the business I'd seen showed *The Trump* had yet to turn a profit, although advertising was picking up.

"I'd like introduce Ann Meadows," said Stella. "As you know, Ann will be our go-to person for background."

There was a chorus of hellos. Stella named each reporter for me. "Brad you've met. Beside him is Francesca Marsh. Then

Alec Slater and Jon Hong. I'll leave you all to get acquainted."
Without further ceremony, she left the room.

Brad flashed his excellent teeth at me. "Coffee, Ann?"

"Thank you. Black, no sugar." I gave the others a polite
smile. Although I'd read each person's file, and knew more
about them than they could imagine, I said, "I'm so sorry, but
I'm not particularly good with names, and Ms. Rohm reeled
them off so quickly . . ."

"I'm Jon," said Jon Hong. "Looking forward to working
with you."

His parents had migrated from Hong Kong when he'd been
a toddler. He had a slight build, straight, inky black hair worn
quite long and smooth brown skin. Jon had been brought up a
Roman Catholic and attended Mass almost every morning. His
free time was largely taken up with an outreach youth program
run by his church. Somewhat oddly, given these circumstances,
Jon Hong was engaged to marry a devout young Muslim
woman. I didn't think it fair, but the simple fact he had a close
relationship with someone of the Muslim faith had occasioned
a much more concentrated examination of his life and contacts.
So far nothing incriminating had been found.

A balding, bulky man with little piggy eyes came over and
seized my hand. "Alec," he said, radiating good cheer. "Alec
Slater. Perhaps you've noticed my byline?"

He had a slick, friendly manner, rather like a successful tele-
vangelist. This disguised the killer shark beneath. The information I had depicted him as an excellent journalist, but a ruthless
one who'd do anything to get a story and who had a reputation
for claiming full credit for investigative items when other, more
junior reporters had done most of the work.

As I murmured something to Alec Slater about admiring the
depth of his research, the only woman on the team, Francesca
Marsh, gave a scornful laugh. "Yeah, right!" she said.

Alec's friendly veneer disappeared. "Fran, you superior bitch," he snarled, "you can drop the holier-than-thou attitude. I seem to remember a little matter of plagiarism in your resume."

She shot him a venomous look. "I was set up, you bastard, and you know it."

If so, she'd set herself up. While working under the name Fran Coulter for another major newspaper, Francesca Marsh had lifted, without attribution, a considerable portion of an article detailing the ineffective responses of government bodies to the challenges of natural disasters over the past twenty-five years. The article she'd stolen from had been published in an obscure ecological journal with a readership of only a few thousand. Unfortunately Francesca Marsh had been unlucky enough to have one of those readers recognize the borrowed material. Although she denied everything, the evidence was damning, and when other unacknowledged borrowings had been discovered in her work, she'd been fired.

She'd reinvented herself as Francesca Marsh by reverting to the full form of her first name and using her married surname, Marsh. Apparently Jason Benton was willing to overlook her fall from grace. This could be because the adjective that came to mind when looking at Francesca was "voluptuous."

She had a full, ripe body with wide hips and heavy breasts. Her thick, red-gold hair fell to her shoulders. She wasn't beautiful, but had a striking face, each feature exaggerated so that her mouth was wider, her nose more emphatic, her eyes more lustrous than any ordinary mortal.

Although Francesca exuded an undeniable eroticism, she'd been married to the same man—of all things, an accountant—for twelve years and had three children. There may have been disgrace in her professional career, but there wasn't even a whisper of scandal about her private life.

I became aware she was examining me closely. "I'm guessing you're a conformist, Ann. Would I be right?"

"If you mean do I espouse traditional values," I said, lifting my chin, "then yes, I'm a conformist and proud to be called so."

Brad beamed at me. "It's like convent girls. Straight and narrow all the way, but then, when they kick over the traces, look out! Bacchanalia!"

"That's a rather passé concept, I'm afraid," I said, my distaste plain. I put my pale blue briefcase on the table and snapped the locks open. "I have some material here that may be of use. My first official day is tomorrow, and we can discuss any points you might want amplified then."

After handing out the sheets, I closed my briefcase, bestowed a well-mannered smile on the four of them, said, "Until tomorrow," and exited the conference room. As I closed the door behind me, I heard Francesca say mockingly, "A rather passé concept, I'm afraid!" and then a ripple of laughter.

I was confident I'd fooled them all. Cynthia—I gave myself a mental shake—*Courtney* would be pleased with me.

I was looking forward to meeting Emmaline Partlow with both curiosity and trepidation. My instructions were to gain her confidence and, if I judged it useful, to become involved with her religious movement. She was, by all accounts, a formidable woman, who had founded Supremity and then managed to sell the concept to a multitude of ardent followers, almost all of whom were blessed with high incomes.

As part of my preparation, I'd studied the Supremity movement. It had the three attributes of an effective religion or cult. First, there were holy scriptures, which believers were required to accept as speaking with absolute authority. The Bible or the

Koran were examples in major religions. In Supremity's case, the holy scriptures were *The Supremity Chronicles*, made up of the inspired writings of Emmaline Partlow who claimed the words had been dictated to her by an ultimate being existing in another higher dimension.

Second, there were learned interpreters of the scriptures who studied the sacred texts and then made pronouncements as to their meaning. The main role here was taken by Professor Angus Finn, previously a world-renowned authority on comparative religions, but now a self-styled "Professor of Supremity" who had made his life's work the study of *The Chronicles*.

The third requirement was a priesthood with special powers and privileges. For Supremity, this consisted of Emmaline Partlow at the top, assisted by her Council of the Paramount, three individuals selected by Emmaline as being at the peak of spiritual evolution.

Somehow ASIO researchers had obtained an annotated copy of *The Supremity Chronicles*. I didn't have the time or the inclination to wade through the volume, which was written in flowery language, but I skimmed it to get an impression of the contents. Bound in gold leather, it was printed on heavy, parchment-like paper. Emmaline Partlow had incorporated elements from, among others, the teachings of Gurdjieff, Madame Blavatsky's Theosophy and the Rosicrucian Order. In essence, *The Chronicles* maintained that those drawn to embrace Supremity were to consider themselves superior to ordinary people. Their wealth and position in the world already demonstrated this, but within each person was a spark of divinity that, when properly fueled with knowledge gained through close study of *The Supremity Chronicles*, would flare up, illuminating the hidden truths of life and enabling each follower to achieve his or her true potential in both the material and spiritual spheres. And, of course, ultimately to pass on to a higher plane of existence, reserved for the truly excellent.

Supremity had leased a city penthouse overlooking the Sydney Harbour Bridge and the Opera House. When giving me directions to the exclusive apartment building, Lorna Gosling had indicated that there would be other guests, but she was not at liberty to say who they might be. "For security," she'd murmured, as though someone might be listening. "Emmaline insists on tight security."

"I suppose that's wise."

Lorna had looked at me, wide-eyed. "Can you imagine, there are actually people who would hurt Emmaline? And she's done so much good for the world . . ."

The dinner party tonight would be my first real test. It was important to make the right impression, so I dressed with the care Ann Meadows would use, choosing a simple pale green dress and slightly higher heels than for daytime wear. Naturally Ann would make sure shoes and handbag matched and would select a pearl necklace and a dainty silver bracelet. I usually wore minimal makeup, but for this role I spent some time in front of the mirror.

I squinted at my elegant little watch, which had a face so ridiculously small one could only make an educated guess as to the time. I didn't intend to be fashionably late. At eight sharp I'd be at the penthouse door.

The drive was quite eventful, as Sydney streets seemed to be continually changing to accommodate the tunnels that carried traffic underneath the city. Fortunately I'd given myself some leeway, because I had to take a circuitous route to get to my destination. It was immediately obvious the building had excellent security. I wasn't permitted into the underground parking area until proof of my identity was closely examined. I knew from the moment I got out of my car I was under surveillance. In the lobby two guards viewed my driving license and credit cards, made sure I wasn't carrying a weapon in my bag and compared my name with a list of guests. Then one called up to announce my arrival while the other escorted me to the lift and punched in a code to activate it. The doors hissed closed and I was alone except for the inconspicuous lens of the video camera surveying me.

I stood neatly, feet together, back straight, expression serious. A woman of refinement, who could be trusted not to rock the boat. The real me would be tempted to make a rude face at the camera, but my alter ego ignored it as though she didn't realize its single, unblinking eye was trained on her.

Accompanied by a hulking man in a dark suit, Emmaline Partlow herself met me when I stepped out of the lift into a small, unfurnished area, the walls, floor and ceiling of which were the same lavender color. Her solid build was swathed in a diaphanous purple outfit, which fell in billowing panels to the floor. She had a square face and strong jaw line and wore her silvery hair in a pageboy bob. Her eyes were her best feature— very dark, magnetic and heavy-lidded.

"Ann Meadows," she said in a low, husky voice with a trace of a Southern accent, which was appropriate, since she'd been born in Louisiana. "You are the first of my guests to arrive."

I inclined my head in acknowledgement. "Ms. Partlow."

She frowned. "Emmaline, please. Formal address merely hides the true self."

"Emmaline," I repeated obediently.

I glanced over at the man, who had positioned himself against the wall, his face expressionless, but she made no move to introduce him. She was fully occupied directing a piercing stare at me, as if seeing something untoward.

I raised my eyebrows. "Is something wrong?"

"There is duplicity in your aura."

"I beg your pardon?"

Impatience crossed Emmaline's face. "Sensitives such as myself are able to discern the subtle emanation surrounding each living creature—the aura."

"And you can see mine?"

"Very clearly. And its colors are indicating duplicity, deceit."

I recalled Stella's words this afternoon: "She's like a human lie detector." My skin prickled in a superstitious response even as I reassured myself Emmaline Partlow couldn't possibly see auras. This was just an attempt to unbalance me. She probably did something like this with every new person she met in order to establish her other-worldly credentials.

"What colors?" I asked.

"Several, including a muddy brown." With a look of regret, she added, "Not a good sign, I'm afraid."

"Deception has been my career for many years," I said. "Could this be the explanation?"

She considered, then nodded. "It may very well be your time in the intelligence world has affected your aura adversely." Without looking behind her, she snapped her fingers, "Kenny?" With slow, deliberate steps, he walked over to us.

"This is Kenny," she said. "He looks after my personal security."

"A bodyguard?" I sounded surprised, although I'd been well briefed on Kenny Dowd.

Emmaline clasped her hands. "We live in perilous times, Ann, perilous times. I'm afraid I'm sometimes the target of vicious attacks. These are, praise the Great Spirit, usually verbal or written, but there have been a couple of instances where Kenny has literally saved my life."

He was heavy-shouldered, going slightly to fat, and walked with a flat, intimidating tread. He had regular, unremarkable features, sandy hair receding fast and a relentless movement of his jaws as he constantly chewed gum.

Kenny Dowd had been a professional football player in the States. He'd only lasted one season, then retired with a career-ending knee injury. Then he'd had several years with the New York Police Department, resigning before a career-ending accusation of corruption had been lodged against him. He'd been on the Supremity payroll for five years, first in charge of general security, but for the last three as Emmaline Partlow's personal bodyguard. So far he'd made no career-ending mistakes on this job.

"How do you do?" I said, holding out my hand to him.

He gave me a perfunctory handshake, but a least he stopped chewing for a moment. "Fine," he got out. "I'm fine," before his jaws started up again.

Emmaline looked amused. "Kenny's a man of few words, but in action, he has no equal."

I looked to see if she could possibly be making some reference to Kenny's sexual prowess, but it seemed not, as her expression was bland.

"Can you see the color of your own aura? And Kenny's?" I inquired.

"One's aura is an intensely private aspect of one's wholeness," she said sternly, "so I can make no comment on Kenny's, but as for myself"—a satisfied smile curved her lips—"as a highly evolved being, my aura is a pure violet, crowned with a radiant aureole of brilliant white light."

"A halo, you mean?" My tone was respectful, with a touch of awe.

"Precisely, Ann," she said approvingly. "I sense your mystical potential is as yet untapped."

With a self-deprecating smile, I said, "I'm not sure I have any mystical potential. I'm a very practical person."

Emmaline put a reassuring hand on my arm. "Trust me,

Ann. I see in you an as yet unplumbed depth of spirituality. If you were to undertake cleansing of your aura through the Supremity purification protocol, your psychic self would be freed and your sixth sense activated."

"Supremity could do that?" I put a note of doubt in my voice.

"That and more. I know it seems incredible, but the world is more than we know." She leaned forward confidingly. "We must speak of this later, in depth."

I felt a shiver of alarm. This was entirely too easy. Was it a trap?

My expression, I was certain, showed nothing but thoughtful interest, but Emmaline, smiling benignly, said, "You're not to be apprehensive, Ann. Your secrets—all of them—will be safe with me."

CHAPTER EIGHT

"I have a question," I said as Emmaline still held my arm and led me through an archway into the penthouse with Kenny following close behind.

"Perhaps you're wondering, Ann, why I invited you here tonight."

"That's amazing," I said, actually feeling taken aback, as it was the question I was about to ask. "How did you know?"

With a sphinx smile, Emmaline said, "Supremity teaches us how to cross the boundaries between the physical and the spiritual world. Knowing someone else's thoughts is merely a matter of concentration at the correct vibration."

"It's rather unsettling to find you can read my mind."

"It won't be when you understand it fully. Now, to answer your question. I have the keenest interest in your area of expertise, and I was delighted when Jason mentioned you were joining

The Trump. My mission, as leader of Supremity, is to seek out people who have, whether they realize it or not, the qualities of highly evolved beings. Someone like you, Ann, who has devoted your career to the analysis of momentous secrets, has already demonstrated some of those inestimable qualities."

I looked at her, wondering if she really could believe this total balderdash. Or if she thought that I did. Emmaline gazed back at me serenely. "Let's not talk of it now," she said, "but please consider my words without prejudice or judgment."

I nodded soberly. "All right."

The penthouse took up the entire top floor of the building, and there was a stunning panoramic view of the city and harbor. Emmaline led me through glass doors onto a wide balcony. It was enchanting to look in one direction and see the floodlit curving sails that formed the unique shape of the Sydney Opera House, or to glance back towards the towers of the city and catch sight of the huge arch of the Harbour Bridge.

"It's so beautiful here," I said.

She took my arm again. "Let me show you around."

The penthouse was furnished sumptuously, but everything—furniture, walls, ceiling, carpet—was in shades of lilac, mauve, lavender and violet.

Emmaline looked around approvingly. "You notice the color scheme?"

I felt like exclaiming, "You'd have to be totally blind not to notice this cloying color scheme!" but Ann would not be so impolite. I said, "Is the choice of purple tones of some significance?"

"Indeed, it is of great significance. These colors represent the highest, most spiritual vibrations of the evolved soul. Ask yourself, is it an accident that I, myself, wear purple?"

I repressed a smile at the thought that no one, by accident, could possibly drape her stout body in such a hectic shade. "I suppose not."

"Purple is a royal color, one of divine authority, but also one of sacrifice. I, myself—"

She broke off as Lorna Gosling came hurrying into the room. "Emmaline, Mr. Benton's in the elevator. He'll be here any moment."

Emmaline excused herself, and with purple panels billowing around her, made her way out of the room, her progress making me think of a luxury yacht inexorably cleaving the waves.

Lorna stood irresolutely beside me, obviously not sure whether to follow her employer or stay with me. She'd piled her limp brown hair on top of her head and secured it with a silver clip, but escaping strands gave the impression the hairdo was about to collapse. She was attired in a white tunic and sandals, which made her look like something out of a Roman epic.

"You didn't mention you'd be here this evening, Lorna," I said.

"As a personal assistant, I'm on call 'round the clock," she said with a touch of smugness. "And because there are eight for dinner tonight, Emmaline asked me to help Ivy."

"Ivy?"

"Cook and housekeeper." Lorna's voice held a trace of scorn. "Ivy tends to get a bit flustered when there are more than six at the table."

"So Emmaline entertains a lot?"

Lorna appeared surprised I'd asked such a question. "It's a vital part of Supremity's outreach. Emmaline has the power to lift society to a higher level through her impact upon influential people."

One of those influential people, Jason Benton, was following Emmaline through the door right now. My heart did a flip. Behind Benton was a woman, wearing scarlet. Roanna Aylmer.

I found the dining room oppressive. The same color scheme was repeated. The walls were lavender, the carpet a light purple, the ceiling amethyst, its darker shade seeming to press down into the room. The tablecloth covering the jumbo-sized rectangular dining table was, mercifully, snowy white, although the linen table napkins were an intense purple.

Lorna and Ivy served the first course, a lightly-spiced tomato soup. Ivy had turned out to be a dour, grim type who wore a large white apron over her white tunic and sandals. I had the stray thought that cooking in sandals might be a hazard to one's feet, but clearly it was the uniform Emmaline expected her staff to wear when on duty at the penthouse. I looked over at Kenny, sitting stolidly opposite me, and mentally dressed him in a tunic and sandals.

The tiny, blond woman beside me noticed my private grin. "Enjoying yourself? I am too, *so* much. Emmaline's *so* wonderful, don't you think?"

I gave a noncommittal, "Hmmm."

Her name was Nancy Otega, and she was the speechwriter, PR person and general troubleshooter for rapidly-rising politician Rafe Thorne. Although she gushed artlessly, opened her baby-blue eyes wide and flashed her excellent teeth in charming smiles, I knew her to be a ruthless, effective operator who had elevated media manipulation to an art form.

I glanced around the table. Jason Benton had been given the position of honor at its head. He was as unprepossessing as his photographs. Perhaps he'd been driven to make his mark on the world to compensate for his toad-ugly face and scrawny, hollow-chested body. His suit was beautifully tailored, which made his looks seem all the more incongruous, as though someone so unsightly should be wearing unattractive clothes. He spoke in a monotone, and very softly, so people had to strain to hear him clearly.

Emmaline was sitting at his right hand, talking animatedly to him. Benton nodded every now and then, but his gaze was constantly moving from one guest to another. Roanna had said Benton and Emmaline had been lovers. My imagination grappled unsuccessfully with the images this provoked.

Next to Emmaline, and opposite me, was Kenny Dowd. I wondered if he were bored. He must have sat through countless dinner parties and listened to the same topics, the same empty chatter, evening after evening. His expression was completely blank, although, like Jason Benton, he constantly scanned the room.

Next to Kenny's dark suit, Roanna's scarlet dress glowed, the most brilliant point at the table. She looked ravishingly lovely, and I had to force myself not to stare at her.

Roanna was chatting with Rafe Thorne, who sat at the bottom of the table. Only a year or so ago, he'd been an insignificant federal politician, who had been voted into his seat by chance it seemed when his opponent, assured of victory in the polls, had suddenly died while playing golf. Now Rafe Thorne was the leader of the fastest-growing political party in the nation, Right Way.

At first mocked by established parties, Right Way was gaining adherents and amassing money at an amazing rate. Like other right-wing splinter groups, Right Way tapped into the discontent and resentment of the have-nots who found purpose and meaning in finding someone to blame for their unsatisfactory position in the world. In the next federal elections Right Way candidates were deemed likely to substantially increase the number of seats the party held.

"The right way for Australia is the Right Way! Drive the interlopers from our nation! Reclaim our country!" was

69

Thorne's initial rallying cry, and the disaffected flocked to join the movement. As it gained in strength, Right Way's rhetoric became harsher and more direct:

"Purify Australia!"

"Deport, deport, deport . . . it's the Right Way."

Supporters agreed fully with Thorne's assertion that Australia belonged to those he called, "The descendants of the first settlers." Ignoring the uncomfortable fact that the first settlers were actually the Aboriginal people, forty thousand or more years ago, Right Way followers correctly took Thorne's statement as shorthand for: *British or Irish heritage and most definitely white.*

Rafe Thorne was close to the perfect politician. He was tall and well-built, had a rich, mellifluous voice, thick black hair with a touch of gray at the temples, twinkling blue eyes, a not-too-handsome face with a resolute jaw. In his youth he'd played cricket and football, and still claimed a keen interest in sport. He made a point of not being overeducated: "I'm an ordinary, down-to-earth Aussie who loves his country deeply. I speak for the regular, salt-of-the-earth citizen, ignored by the silver-tongued career politicians. I give voice to the patriots who want Australia for the Australians."

"Have you met Rafe before?" Nancy Otega asked me.

"Not until this evening."

She gave me a guileless smile. "And what do you think of Right Way?"

"I don't have an opinion. I'm not into politics."

"You're not? Really?" said Nancy ingenuously. "But you're an intelligence expert, aren't you? Isn't your job to know all about political movements?"

"That's why I have no opinion one way or the other," I said primly. "You might call it a professional stance."

"Really?" she said again. She turned to her left to pluck at

Rafe Thorne's sleeve. "Rafe! Ann here has no opinion about Right Way. No opinion at all."

"Indeed?" he said, tearing his attention away from Roanna and bestowing on me a warm, sincere politician's smile. "I must do something about that, Ann. I'd very much like to talk with you later." He put up a well-manicured hand. "Not that I'm recruiting for members. Don't worry about that. But I'd welcome a chance to discuss Right Way with you."

I gave a rote reply. "I look forward to it."

First Emmaline, now Rafe Thorne wanted to speak with me later. I was set up to be indoctrinated spiritually and politically. My glance strayed to Roanna. What about the physical sphere?

I resolutely shook that thought off as the eighth person at the table, Oliver Yorkin, began to tell me and anyone else who'd listen a long, elaborate joke about suicide bombers. It was difficult, I thought, to find anything amusing about such people, but Oliver did his best.

Oliver Yorkin, managing editor-opinion at *The Trump*, was a bouncy little man, almost completely bald, with only a fringe of hair left above his ears. He had a booming, unmodulated voice, and an extraordinary, wheezing laugh, which he was employing now after delivering the joke's punch line.

"Get it? Paradise was closed that day?" He shook his head in wonderment. "Closed for the day! Funny, eh?"

"Very droll," I said.

He gave me a pained look. "Droll? That's dismissive. I don't believe you got the point at all."

"Don't badger Ann," said Emmaline from the other side of the table. "She's just joined *The Trump* and doesn't yet understand your ways, Oliver."

For no reason I could see, Oliver seemed to find her comment hilarious, and the table was treated to another asthmatic, braying laugh.

At the head of the table, Jason Benton snapped shut the phone he'd been using and slipped it into his jacket pocket. Then he said something, obviously directed at all of us.

"Oh, Jason, we can't hear you down at this end," Nancy Otega said, clasping her hands in fake distress. Everyone stopped speaking and looked at him.

"I said, there's been another sniper attack this evening at a fast food outlet in Penrith. A toddler and her father killed. Excellent material for a human interest slant. Francesca Marsh and Jon Hong are covering the story."

"Fucking Righteous Scourge," snapped Oliver, clearly outraged. His face flushed, he went on, "What do you think the going rate is for little kids? A hundred thousand, plus a bonus for the dad?"

"Why? That's what I ask," declared Emmaline Partlow. "Why would the Righteous Scourge people be funding these attacks? What's in it for them? What do they hope to achieve?"

"We don't know if they *are* funding them," said Roanna. "It could be a confidence trick. Arrive in the Cayman Islands, ask for your money, and find out it's not there. To whom do you complain? The cops? I don't think so."

"Fear and panic," said Jason Benton in his soft monotone. "That's what they hope to achieve. Get the general public stirred up, so they demand answers."

"But to what end?" Emmaline asked. "I mean, what's the ultimate goal?"

This was a question much debated in the intelligence community. Urban terrorism through the ages had had as its broad purpose, as Jason Benton said, the creation of fear and panic in the general public. Sowing seeds of terror was all very well, but to what specific purpose? Encouraging these uncoordinated attacks from would-be terrorists of varying skills, was a piecemeal approach. Why not have one large, spectacular hit, such as the destruction of the World Trade Center and the Pentagon? These highly visual attacks left iconic images of planes flying into tall buildings forever etched on the memory of anyone who watched the media coverage.

"To bring the federal government down." Rafe Thorne, looking every inch a leader, surveyed the table. "It's political. It's always been political."

"The prime minister is looking increasingly shaky," I observed. "I get the feeling his deputy is eyeing his position."

"Changing hands at the helm while the ship is sinking?" said Rafe Thorne with deep scorn, his strong jaw jutting. "It's not enough. The whole corrupt edifice has to fall. We need to sweep this weak, prevaricating government out of power."

Nancy chimed in with, "The people of Australia must demand a general election. Absolutely demand it."

Thorne looked down the length of the table to Jason Benton. "What do you say, Jason?"

Benton tented his hands and considered the question. No one made a sound. At last he spoke. "I say *The Austral Trumpeter* is behind you Rafe. Behind you all the way."

I got home to my little flat after one, mentally and physically drained. The discussion around the table had turned to specific examples of the inability of the present administration to respond meaningfully to the terrorist attacks and what they could, or should have done. Doubts were expressed about the ability of the opposition, if they took power, to do much better. As I was the resident authority on terrorism, many questions had been directed at me.

It was truly ironic. In reality, I was an intelligence officer, and here I was, undercover, playing an intelligence officer. Even so, I was surrounded by sharp minds and maintaining Ann

Meadows persona, while dealing adequately with every query thrown my way, had been exhausting.

I'd changed into my pajamas, cleaned my teeth and was ready to fall into bed when the front doorbell chimed. I checked the security monitor and my pulse jumped.

Wrenching open the door, I said, "What are you doing here, Roanna?"

"I couldn't stay away."

"We can't be seen together. Just go."

She stepped into the little hallway. "Don't shut me out, Denise."

Torn between rage that she'd so thoughtlessly compromised my assignment, and a sudden, overwhelming surge of desire, I said, "Leave, please."

"You don't mean that." She shut the door and locked it. "Do you?"

CHAPTER NINE

Roanna had changed from her scarlet dress into jeans and a tight white T-shirt. She wasn't wearing a bra, and my eyes were drawn to the clear outline of her nipples. She smiled at me. "See how much I want you, darling?"

"How did you get this address?"

"Simple. I'm a computer expert, remember? Not that it needed much skill to access *The Trump's* personnel files. I was visiting the newsroom and simply slipped into someone's cubicle when it was free."

"Roanna, this is stupid and unprofessional. You're jeopardizing my cover."

"Nobody will know anything about it. Jason dropped me back at my hotel, I went up to my room, changed, then drove over here. It's a rental car, so it can't easily be traced to me."

"You being here is an unacceptable risk."

She stepped forward and put her arms around me. "You look incredibly sexy in those pale blue pajamas."

That got a reluctant smile from me. "You're kidding, right?"

"But you'd look a whole lot sexier without them."

I didn't want to kiss her. I didn't want to have her there at all. I should bundle her unceremoniously out the front door and slam it in her face.

"Denise?"

I kissed her and was lost.

Roanna slid her hands under my pajama top. A wave of fire washed over me. I gasped, fighting to rally my willpower, but it had gone down without more than a token whimper.

We were kissing urgently, feverishly. "We can't do this," I said, without conviction.

My knees felt weak. Roanna murmured against my throat, "The couch? The floor? Or bed? You decide—but hurry."

"Bed," I said, a tremor in my voice. "I'm all for comfort."

"It's not comfort that I had in mind."

Roanna was tearing off her T-shirt before we reached the bedroom door. I watched her slide off her jeans. My hands were shaking as I stripped off Ann Meadows's conservative cotton pajamas.

"It's been too long, Denise."

"It seems that way."

Her skin was smooth beneath my hands. My mouth found the hollow of her throat, her breasts, her tanned belly. She moaned as my fingers entered her, and too soon, she climaxed.

Then she was between my legs, and I was rising, rising. At the last moment, before I exploded into flight, I thought of Cynthia.

"You look awfully tired, Ann!"

Lorna Gosling, dressed in a mauve pantsuit, beamed at me,

76

exuding bright-eyed health and energy. I gave her a half-strength glower, all I could manage. "It was a late night."

"You should have come to the gym early this morning with me and Stella. Sets you up for the whole day."

I smothered a yawn. "Thanks for the invitation. I'll think about it."

Lorna bounced into the small cubicle I'd been assigned and perched on the edge of my desk. "Isn't Emmaline wonderful? And she's taking a special, personal interest in you, Ann."

"I'm flattered."

"You should be," she said earnestly. "Usually Emmaline leaves it all to the recruiting team to carry out the initial approach."

"Supremity has a recruiting team?"

"Actually, members are called neophyte gatherers."

"Catchy term," I said.

Lorna apparently didn't detect the sarcastic note in my voice, as she said, "Isn't it! And the gatherers do such important work. We call it soul gathering. Without gatherers, so many people would go through life never realizing that an entire spiritual dimension was missing from their existence."

I contemplated my empty coffee mug. I'd gulped down two, but needed more caffeine desperately having had barely three hours sleep after Roanna had left me, solemnly swearing not to run the risk of meeting this way again.

Tuning back in, I found Lorna was still speaking. " . . . gathering of Roanna herself."

"Sorry, what did you say?"

"I said Mr. Benton asked Emmaline if she would handle the gathering of Roanna herself. Emmaline couldn't say no, because Mr. Benton's a close friend and business partner."

"Why don't you call Benton by his first name?" I asked, curious. "Isn't that what Supremity teaches?"

Lorna shook her head ruefully. "Mr. Benton snapped at me

77

when I called him 'Jason.' He said it was disrespectful to a man in his position."

My eyes watered as I fought another yawn. "How many people at the table last night belong to Supremity?"

Lorna was quite happy to confide the religious affiliations of the guests. "Well, Mr. Benton says he's interested, and he's read *The Chronicles*, but he hasn't fully committed yet. Same for Oliver. He told Emmaline he was brought up a Baptist, but he's willing to keep an open mind—although I don't think he really means it."

"How about Emmaline's bodyguard?"

"Kenny? He got gathered as soon as he took the job. Emmaline wouldn't have employed him, otherwise."

"What about Rafe Thorne?"

"Oh, he's been in Supremity for ages. He was one of the first in Australia to join. He's next in line for when a vacancy occurs in the Council of the Paramount."

"Strange," I said, "I've never seen it mentioned anywhere that Rafe Thorne belongs to Supremity."

Lorna bit her lip. "You'll keep it quiet, won't you?"

"Of course, but why is it a secret?"

"Not everyone is open-minded about Supremity. We've even been called a cult, like we're some crazy religious sect!"

I tut-tutted. "Hard to believe," I said.

"So Emmaline says sometimes it's better for people of particular influence to keep their membership secret."

"I guess his PR woman makes sure Thorne's name is never linked to Supremity."

A shadow darkened Lorna's face. "Nancy Otega? She'd be happy to have Rafe leave Supremity altogether and ruin his immortal soul. You can't have a rational discussion with her. She's full of mockery and scorn." Lorna dropped her voice to add, "I think Nancy's an *atheist*. No spiritual dimension at all."

"Clearly she could do with a bit of stern soul gathering," I said.

Lorna frowned at me. I was beginning to suspect she had no sense of humor. Too late I realized Ann Meadows didn't have one either. "I'm not trying to be funny," I said hastily.

"Hate to interrupt your girls' talk," said Alec Slater, sticking his balding head over the partition between my cubicle and his, "but Stella's called a meeting in the conference room. Starting now."

"Okay," I said, getting up.

Alec gave Lorna a lascivious grin. "And how's Emmaline's little vestal virgin this morning?"

Not surprisingly, Lorna bristled. "You have an undeveloped soul," she observed coldly.

Alec chuckled suggestively. "That may be, sweetheart, but I guarantee you won't be disappointed with my development in other areas."

"Excuse me." Lorna left, head held high.

"Can't take a joke," said Alec. "Those religious types never can." He winked at me. "How about you?"

"I don't find many things amusing," I said in a suitably frosty tone. "Shall we go to the meeting?"

When Alec and I entered the conference room, Francesca, Jon Hong and handsome Brad Thomson were already sprawled in chairs. Jon gave me a worried look, then glanced away. I wondered what that was about, and made a mental note to follow it up.

There were copies of this morning's edition of *The Austral Trumpeter* spread over the conference table. I'd already glanced at the paper while drinking my first mug of newsroom coffee. Francesca and Jon's story had been the front page lead:

SNIPER SLAYS TODDLER, FATHER
OUTRAGE RISES AS PM PROMISES ACTION

"The prime minister promises action!" said Stella Rohm, striding into the room and jabbing at the closest copy of the paper. "What action? We've got to pin the bastard down. Vague generalizations won't do."

She looked around, a commandant marshaling her troops. "Right! Here are your assignments . . ." In staccato fashion, she handed out tasks for each member of the team. The prime minister was in Sydney, and Alec and Francesca were to cover his media conference this afternoon. "I shouldn't need to remind you to ask short, unambiguous questions. There'll be competition, but Alec, I can rely on you to get in early. I want to hear your voice first on the TV coverage. Francesca, back him up—cut off anyone trying to interrupt. And don't let the PM waffle. Hold his feet to the fire. Nail him!"

"A pleasure," said Alec.

Brad was to follow up on last night's murder of the toddler and father. "The TV sharks will be feeding on this one, but you can do better. Link it to the other attacks at the gut level. Take Reece with you for photographs. I want weeping family members—the wife, if you can get her. Plus shocked neighbors and friends. The usual. And there'll be local and federal cops on the case. Look for a female officer and use that undeniable charm of yours, Brad. If there's information the cops are holding back, find out what it is."

"Anything else?" he said with an ironic smile.

"I'll let you know." Stella turned to me. "Ann, you'll be working with Jon. He's had a hot tip from a source on the street about a seventies radical group that's apparently reformed, and are going for the Righteous Scourge big bucks. We need anything on the intelligence side you can dig up. Assure your contacts no names will be used. 'An informed source' is how we'll attribute it."

"Have you passed on the tip to the authorities?" I asked.

"Not yet. You can do it for us, Ann. Jon will brief you." She clapped her hands. "Okay people, let's get this show on the road."

"Your cubicle or mine?" I said to Jon after the others had left the room.

"Mine," he said. "I've got all the info there."

As we walked down the hallway together, I glanced over at him. So much for the old cliché about the inscrutable oriental gentleman—Jon Hong's troubled face showed very clearly that something was weighing heavily on his mind.

"Something the matter?" I said.

He frowned. "Sort of."

"About this radical group we're researching? There's some problem?"

"No." He hesitated, then said, "Actually, it's something about you."

CHAPTER TEN

It had been set up so that when I ostensibly called DIO from an unsecured phone at the newspaper offices, I'd dial a special number that would always be answered by Tony Scott—actually one of several people who would use that name.

"Tony?" I said. "It's Ann Meadows."

"Ann! Delighted to hear from you. How are things going at *The Trump*? Keeping you busy?"

"I only started work today," I said, "but so far yes, they're keeping me busy."

"Before I forget," said Tony, "I've got a message for you. Hold on while I get it."

While I waited for him to come back to the phone, I felt a shiver of foreboding.

"Ann, sorry to keep you waiting. A friend of yours, June Smythe, is trying to get in touch with you. She says you'll know the number. She'll be home this evening."

There was no June Smythe. The message meant Cynthia/Courtney wanted to speak to me urgently. Perhaps my premonition something was wrong had been well founded. As far as I knew, ASIO didn't have my flat under surveillance, but if she'd learned somehow that I'd not only let Roanna in, but that she'd stayed for several hours, Cynthia would be furious at, if nothing else, my lack of professionalism.

"Thanks, Tony, I'll call her this evening. Now, I've got a question about a radical seventies group known as the Coolangatta Five, plus some information to pass on about them . . ."

Tony took down the details Jon Hong had been given, asked for the name of Jon's source and snorted when I said it was the newspaper's policy to protect all anonymous sources. Then he went to access ASIO's files to ascertain if there was anything unclassified that he could give me as background for the group.

As I waited on the phone, I thought about my earlier conversation with Jon. "What did you mean, something about me?" I'd asked when we'd reached his workspace, a cubicle identical to mine. "Is it that you feel uncomfortable working with someone who's not a news person? Is that it?"

Jon had commandeered a chair from another cubicle for me, then had sat in his own seat, reluctance in every line of him. "I shouldn't have said anything."

"You did say it, so come clean, please."

Looking down at a pen he'd been fiddling with, he said, "It's Supremity. I overheard Lorna Gosling telling Stella about how Emmaline Partlow has her eye on you as a new convert. It's so easy to be sucked into the whole cult thing. I've seen it happen before."

When I didn't respond, he looked up. "Look, Ann, I've got strong religious beliefs. My faith teaches me to combat evil, and I see it as my duty to warn you about Supremity. It doesn't measure up against any of the great religions. It's a trendy sect, and its surface attractiveness hides a darkness at its core."

"Hasn't Emmaline Partlow bankrolled *The Trump*? That means you're working for an organization that's largely funded by Supremity."

He'd given me a long, level look. "You don't defeat evil by running away from it."

Nothing more was said on the matter, and we'd gone on to discuss the Coolangatta Five. I wasn't familiar with the name, but Jon had researched enough to know that for a short time they'd been very effective in publicizing their opposition to the war in Vietnam where thousands of Aussie troops had been drafted to fight beside the much larger American forces.

Arson had been the Coolangatta Five's weapon of choice, and their attempts to burn down government buildings, army recruiting centers and the like had been sporadically successful.

No one belonging to the group had ever been caught, and the reason for the name Coolangatta Five was unknown. Whoever they were, they'd gone to ground after their most spectacular attack, directed at a military base. A petrol tanker, fully loaded, had been exploded at an adjacent service station while delivering fuel. The resulting inferno had eventually destroyed more than thirty structures, killed six and wounded more than twenty.

The ASIO agent calling himself Tony came back on the line. "Give me the fax number there," he said. "I'll double-check before I send it, but it looks like enough unclassified material to keep you happy."

The material "Tony Scott" faxed was excellent. It not only covered the Coolangatta Five but cross-referenced similar groups in Australia who'd waged their own small-scale forms of urban terrorism over the past thirty years. Many members of such units had been arrested and charged with various crimes.

The majority had served prison time. ASIO had supplied psycho-social profiles of some of the more interesting participants and had even followed up certain individuals over the years.

After he'd read through the pages, Jon was very enthusiastic. He took me along with him to Stella's office to support an idea the ASIO material had sparked.

"I've got an angle," he said.

Stella leaned back in her chair. "Go on."

He explained what was in the ASIO material. "Most of these dissident groups were pretty ineffectual, but now and then a number did, like the Coolangatta Five, pull off something spectacular."

Stella drummed her fingers on her desk. "So?"

"I'm thinking of an article—maybe a series—examining what it is that causes apparently ordinary individuals to get involved with these anti-establishment movements, where they become potentially deadly activists. Ann says she can get me more detailed info on selected groups." He looked over at me and I nodded on cue.

He went on, "I was thinking of calling it 'Foes of Freedom,' or maybe 'When Freedom Fails,' but of course I'm open to suggestions."

"Both of those suck," said Stella, "but I do like the overall concept. Get back to me with something concrete, and I'll consider it."

Stella's phone rang. She snatched it up, waving Jon off. I turned to follow him out of the office, but Stella said into the receiver, "Hold just a minute." Covering the mouthpiece, she said, "Ann, if you'd stay a moment? I won't be long."

She went back to her call. From her end I gathered someone was trying, with limited success, to pitch a freelance article on Righteous Scourge.

To entertain myself, I looked around the office. There was nothing of interest. No photographs, no awards, no silly souvenirs. Her desk top was uncluttered, except for a PC and monitor. The woman herself, I decided, was uncluttered too. Lithe, tanned, direct. Her short blond hair required little maintenance, and if she wore makeup, I couldn't detect it. Stella Rohm had divorced her husband ten years ago. Her only child, a teenage son, was installed at an exclusive boarding school.

She finished her call from the freelance writer with, "Send it to me. I'll look at it. No promises."

Putting down the receiver with a decisive click, she said, "Lorna tells me you're keen to join us at the gym."

"She did? I'm afraid I didn't say that."

"You're not interested?" Stella looked me up and down. "You look fit, but of course that means nothing. Do you play sport?"

"A little golf," I said, "when I have time."

"Golf?" Stella's expression was close to disgust. "As they say, a good walk spoiled."

"I fail to see—"

"Emmaline Partlow will be inviting you to spend this coming weekend at Supremity Sanctuary. The Esses, as we call it, has a fully equipped gym, indoor swimming pool and spa. You'll be expected to utilize these facilities, so I'll see you there. Be warned: Emmaline will give you a tedious lecture on the importance of a healthy body providing the housing for a healthy soul."

I raised my eyebrows. "I wasn't aware you belonged to Supremity."

Stella gave a short, sardonic laugh. "I don't belong, and I can't imagine ever buying into that pseudo-religious stuff. However, for career reasons, I've decided it's politic for me to remain a seeker after spiritual truths."

"So Emmaline has plans to convert you?"

"She has plans to convert everybody—everybody suitable, that is."

"What makes a person suitable?"

Her phone rang. Before she picked it up, she said, "You should know. She's gung-ho about converting you."

Stella had been correct about the invitation, although it was more of a command. Mid-afternoon, I was summoned to Emmaline's sumptuous office. Today she was wearing a very light lilac outfit, rather more tailored than her purple robes last night.

"You've heard of Supremity Sanctuary?"

She clearly had no doubt I'd read at least some of the enthusiastic articles Supremity's PR firm had planted in various publications, or perhaps watched the breathless Sanctuary tour on TV where a gushing broadcast personality had swooped from room to room, exclaiming over the wonder of the architecture and furnishings.

"I have. It's in the country, isn't it?"

"Only a few hours from Sydney. Your invitation—which, incidentally, is only extended to a select few—is for this weekend." Apparently Emmaline didn't even consider I might refuse, as she added, "Lorna will provide you with directions, or, if you prefer, you may come with me in my limousine."

The more time I spent in her company, the more I might discover. "Oh, that's so very kind of you, Emmaline. I must confess I feel a little overwhelmed by your generosity."

In actual fact, I was suspicious, not overwhelmed. Stella had commented how keen Emmaline was to convert me to Supremity. I wondered why me, in particular. Was it Ann Meadows's background in intelligence? Was that enough to justify this special attention?

"Lorna is presently working on your personalized Sanctuary schedule, commencing with 'Through Grief to Joy,' I believe."

I frowned my puzzlement. "What is that?"

"Ann, I know you've recently lost your husband after a long, lingering illness and still must be deeply grieving."

I'd almost forgotten about my fictitious husband's drawn-out demise. "I try to put it out of my mind," I said bravely.

Emmaline shook her head. "A way of coping, but not one I recommend. The individual's psyche is much damaged by such repression. Physiological and psychological problems can rack the body and mind."

"Do you really think so? I have been sleeping badly, and sometimes feel very low . . ."

"'Through Grief to Joy' is exactly what you need."

"I don't suppose it could hurt." When Emmaline frowned, I added quickly, "If you recommend it, Emmaline, of course I'll be happy to do the course."

"Excellent. Now, I want to talk to you about the importance of a healthy body providing the housing for a healthy soul . . ."

I got home to my little flat, looked at the phone and found reasons not to pick it up. After I'd prevaricated for twenty minutes, I said "To hell with it!" to myself, and dialed the number.

"Courtney? It's Ann." Although we both knew it was a secure connection, the protocol was always maintained to minimize slips if contact had to be made on open lines.

"Ann."

She only said that one word, but her voice was glacial.

During the day I'd brooded over it and decided to tell Cynthia about Roanna, unless she already knew. From her tone, it appeared she did.

"I'm sorry," I said. "It was my poor judgment."

"It was a little more than that, wasn't it? She was in your flat for several hours."

I felt myself blushing, and was angry that I was embarrassed. I demanded, "How did you know?"

"The FBI."

Astonished, I repeated, "The FBI?"

I knew the Federal Bureau of Investigation had a legal attaché in Canberra, and had recently established an attaché in the American consulate in Sydney as part of counterterrorism cooperative measures between the two countries. Surveillance was not part of the agreement.

Cynthia snapped, "You're not the target. She is."

The FBI and Roanna? "They're following Roanna? Why?"

"I can't provide details but use your imagination."

"The Aylmers and their terrorist activities? Something to do with that?"

"In part, yes."

I couldn't believe it. Surely I'd have noticed something that would have told me Roanna wasn't to be trusted. "But why would Roanna bring information to ASIO that might lead to Righteous Scourge? Why help us if she's some way involved in terror campaigns?"

"One excellent reason would be to send us off onto the wrong track by providing fabricated information. Another would be to give herself some insurance to bolster her position if she's arrested. 'I'm helping my country's intelligence services,' she'll say. 'So how can I be a conspirator?'"

"Do you know if the FBI has anything concrete?" I asked.

"I can't discuss what they do or don't have, however, from this moment on you're to treat Roanna Aylmer as a serious security risk." Cynthia paused, then added acidly, "No pillow talk, Ann. In fact, no more intimacy of any kind, if you can manage that."

The best way to salvage something from this horrible conversation was to be businesslike. "Understood," I said. "May I give you my report now?"

There was a pause. Then in a less confrontational tone, Cynthia said, "The message to call me was about something else."

"What?" It had to be important.

"Let's debrief you first, then I'll tell you."

Everything I said would be recorded and later put in written form. I made my report succinctly, touching on everything that had happened since I'd arrived in Sydney—everything except my romantic interlude with Roanna. As a topic for discussion that was permanently off-limits, I hoped.

I concluded with the fact I was to be Emmaline Partlow's guest at Supremity Sanctuary this coming weekend.

"That's it," I said. "So what do you need to tell me?"

"Your brother's in hospital," she said.

"Martin? Is it serious?"

"Car accident. He's on life support."

Martin, the brother I hadn't seen for years. "Then it is serious?"

"Very."

CHAPTER ELEVEN

Martin and I had never been close. It wasn't just that he was much older, it was essentially a clash of temperaments. Unfortunately everything I said and did was diametrically opposed to his view of how a kid sister should behave. I was a risk-taker. Martin was staid and conservative. He lectured me. I didn't pay any attention to his advice.

Our mother had died when I was twelve, leaving my father paralyzed with grief. Martin had seen it his role to step into the breach and see to it that I was brought up with the correct values and behaviors. I resented him, and he resented my resentment.

After Father died, there was really very little reason for us to see each other. We kept in touch in a desultory fashion, but as time went on, we essentially became strangers.

As soon as I finished the call to Cynthia, I found myself

unaccountably upset. Martin and I had grown apart, but he was my brother, and however ham-fistedly, after Mum had died he'd done his best to help bring me up.

I dialed the hospital. The only information I could obtain was that Martin Cleever was "resting comfortably" and receiving no visitors except for next of kin. Cynthia had agreed that the circumstances justified the risk I'd take in visiting Martin, even though I'd be forced to use my real identity to establish I was a close family member. I thought ruefully the hospital would have to take my word for it, as I had absolutely nothing with me to prove I was Denise Cleever.

I didn't need to consult a street directory. I was familiar with the hospital—in my wild youth I ended up in the emergency room there after I'd managed to skid a motorcycle into a tree. Taking all the evasive moves to make sure my car wasn't followed took me some time, so it was after nine when I parked and made my way through the sliding glass doors into a medical world that always made me feel on edge. I disliked the antiseptic-and-floor-polish smell of hospitals, the hushed voices and the sense that in the white rooms so many patients were feeling discomfort and distress.

"Denise! Thank God they found you." Martin's wife, Pam, dressed in a rumpled sweat suit, started up from her chair in the intensive care sitting room and gave me a quick, obligatory hug. "The only number I had was your home in Canberra. I left messages, but when you didn't get back to me, I had the bright idea of calling ASIO. They said they'd track you down."

This was my brother's second wife. Martin's first marriage had been to a thin, perpetually whiny young woman who wore the latest fashions. Pam was another type altogether, being rather plump and motherly, with a dress sense to match.

The few times we'd met I'd found her very pleasant—too nice for Martin, I recall thinking. I'd been forced to be a brides-

92

maid at Martin's first wedding, but for his second I was simply a guest. I had been on assignment at the time, and couldn't attend, so I'd sent a suitably expensive gift and received a standard thank you note in return.

"What happened?" I asked, perching on the nearest chair. Cynthia had had only the sketchiest details.

Pam sat down and leaned forward. She looked sick with fatigue. "Martin's been working so hard to build up the business . . . you know he's struck out on his own, don't you?"

I didn't, but nodded affirmatively.

"He's been working late for weeks. Last night it was after midnight when he left the office. Driving home, Martin must have fallen asleep at the wheel. He ran off the road and crashed into one of those huge metal light poles."

"He was driving a Volvo?"

Pam smiled faintly. "Could you doubt it? As far as I know, that's the only sort of car he's ever owned. And thank heavens he was in a Volvo, otherwise he'd be dead."

My brother had lectured me a thousand times about the superior safety record Volvos enjoyed. I knew it was the real reason I'd always had an irrational dislike of the brand.

"What are his injuries?"

"A fractured skull—that's the worst—and broken nose, broken ribs, a dislocated shoulder, cuts and bruises." She wiped her face with her hands. "He's already had one operation to relieve the pressure on his brain. They're waiting to see if they need to go in again."

Suddenly I wanted to be anywhere but here in this sitting room with walls soaked with anguish and grief. I wanted to be a distant onlooker to tragedy, not one of the players. "Can I see Martin?"

"Of course. I'll go in with you." She put her hand on mine. "Denise, just to prepare you—his face is a mess, and he's hooked

93

up to all these machines. He's in an induced coma to treat the swelling of his brain, so he's unconscious and won't know you're here."

Pam spoke to the nurse, and in we went, me inwardly cringing. It was hushed in the IC unit, except for the beeps and hums of machines and medical monitors. I would never have recognized the figure on the high hospital bed as Martin. A machine breathed rhythmically for him, wires and tubes ran from his motionless body. The little I could see of his face was bruised and swollen.

We stood in silence, Pam and I. Her head was bent—perhaps she was praying. At that moment, Supremity as a religion seemed laughably superficial. I hadn't been to church for a long time, but the comfort of the ceremonies of the Anglican faith came back to me.

I felt tears prick my eyes as I recalled the words of The Order for the Visitation of the Sick our local minister had rumbled out in his bass voice when visiting my dying mother. Remembering a few phrases, I whispered them to myself—and to God, if He was listening.

Back in the waiting room, I swallowed hard to regain my composure. A haggard couple sat together in one corner of the room. Pam greeted them, then came over to me and said softly, "Their daughter was fooling around with friends and fell from a third floor balcony. They're waiting for a final assessment before they agree to turn off life support."

"How awful," I said, thinking how totally inadequate I sounded. But what could one say when faced with human heartbreak like this?

Pam slumped in a chair, her head in her hands. "Denise, I'm so afraid he'll die."

I patted her shoulder. "He won't," I said with more conviction than I felt. "He's getting the best possible care. He'll pull through."

Pam looked up at me. "It's moments like this I regret so much we couldn't have children. With kids, there'd be something left of him in them."

Mute, I patted her shoulder again in a clumsy attempt at comfort. I hadn't known Martin and Pam couldn't conceive. Had I thought of it at all, I would have put it down to Martin's choice of a lifestyle not cluttered up with kids.

"You should go home and get some rest," I said.

She shook her head. "I'll stay. If anything happens, I want to be here." Her mouth trembled. "If the worst happens, if Martin dies, I couldn't bear it if there were only strangers by his side."

I couldn't give Pam a contact number in Sydney—the moment I walked out of the hospital I had to become Ann Meadows again.

"I'll call if there's any change," Pam said.

"I'm sorry, but I'll be traveling and not sure exactly where I'll be, so it's better if I call you."

She gave me a half quizzical look. "Don't you have a cell phone?"

"It's better if I call you," I repeated.

She nodded slowly. "Your job? I see."

I drove back to the flat by a direct route. I doubted I'd been followed to the hospital, evasive tactics or not, as Cynthia had made it clear the FBI was interested in Roanna, not me. And if I had been successfully tailed, the person certainly knew where I was headed now.

I drove around the block once, saw nothing amiss, so came back and parked. Inside, I looked around the mundane little apartment. A weary depression came crashing down on me. Martin had someone to care deeply when he was grievously hurt. If I had been lying there in the IC bed, who would be there for me? Roanna, who might have lied to me and been a traitor, after all? Or Siobhan, always living on the edge of betrayal in strange foreign places with unpronounceable names?

Or Cynthia, who at the moment was so coldly angry with me?

I went to the phone and before I could change my mind, dialed her number, knowing any time of day or night the call would be transferred to wherever she was.

"Courtney?"

"Have you seen your brother?" Her voice was cool.

"Yes."

"You're not calling to say your cover's blown?"

"No."

There was a pause, then Cynthia said, in a slightly warmer tone. "How is he?"

"Martin's wife Pam was at the hospital, and she told me what happened. He crashed his car into a light pole. Severe head injuries, so he's in a medically-induced coma."

"I wish there was something I could say, Ann, but there's nothing that will help, is there?"

My throat closed, and I couldn't speak.

Cynthia said, "Ann?"

Finally I choked out, "I'm sorry. I know I'm going to sound like a baby, but I can't bear it that you're angry with me."

Silence. I heard her take a breath. "Oh, Denise," she said, "I let my personal feelings get in the way. I'm the one who should be sorry."

CHAPTER TWELVE

The rest of the week flew by. I made sure to meet as many of the newspaper's staff as possible, I worked hard at amassing information the reporters could utilize, and I accompanied different members of the team to interviews and media conferences. All of this helped to achieve my purpose, which was to be accepted as just another employee of *The Trump*.

My interaction with the reporters on the team had begun with me seeing them as means to an end, but as I observed them working, my admiration for their achievements grew. All were excellent journalists, fired with a zeal to get the story, and get it right.

On a personal level, my relationships with them varied. Brad Thomson was eternally sunny with everyone, including me, a characteristic that seemed to annoy Alec Slater immeasurably. However, Brad, outgoing as he was, remained an unknown quantity, and his depth, if any existed, was hidden beneath his gregarious exterior.

I could sum up Jon Hong by saying he was an outstandingly nice man. He took his job very seriously and was meticulous in getting every fact and reference correct, but he also had a sweet, mischievous side. Straight-faced, he'd make some witty comment, then wait, not always successfully, for his audience to get it. In a way this was a trial for me, because Ann Meadows was the literal sort who would rarely pick up on a clever quip, so I often had to appear humorless when, as Denise, I would be laughing in appreciation.

Jon was the only one of the team to whom I mentioned the dead reporter, Steven Ivers. "Yes, I knew him. It was tragic how he died."

He seemed puzzled I'd brought the subject up, so I said, "I heard there was talk his death was linked to national security."

Jon looked surprised. "I think you'll find it was Asian gangs. They're totally ruthless, have no respect for human life."

"No one's been arrested."

"And not likely to be," he said somberly. "The gangs have a code of silence that would impress the Mafia."

The one person on the team who clearly disliked me from our first meeting was Francesca Marsh. I didn't particularly like Ann Meadows myself, but in Francesca's place I would have at the least been distantly pleasant. Francesca didn't bother, but then, she didn't appear to warm to any of her own gender. It couldn't be that she saw me as a potential threat in the male-female arena, as she was quite strikingly sensual and, except for Alec Slater, effortlessly charmed any male who came her way.

I found Alec Slater's personality as unattractive as his appearance. Although he had a superficial friendliness, close acquaintance with him revealed Alec's deep dislike of humanity in general and his colleagues in particular. He had a penchant for making sneering comments designed to wound. When challenged, he claimed he was merely joking. Alec and Francesca Marsh clearly loathed each other, but worked together very well.

It was a fascinating time to be working in a newspaper office. The issue of terrorism was challenging the political sphere as never before. The public's fear of the faceless terrorists and their ongoing attacks was allied with a deep and growing dissatisfaction with the government's responses to the threat.

In their reports, Alec and Francesca, along with most of the media, put the prime minister on the metaphorical rack and proceeded to tighten it relentlessly. His approval ratings, falling for several months, began a precipitous slide. There was talk of him standing aside so his deputy could take leadership of the party, thus automatically becoming the new prime minister. The pundits generally agreed this would be a disaster, as the prime minister had been careful to surround himself with political mediocrities unlikely to ever challenge his leadership. This meant there was no one viable to step in, although ambition was driving several in his party to jockey for the position of front-runner.

The first of Jon Hong's articles inspired by the material I'd obtained on the Coolangatta Five and similar groups was to be published in the Saturday edition of *The Trump*. Stella had come up with "Home Grown Horror" for the overall series heading, and although Jon argued fervently for his choice, "Amateur Anarchists," Stella won out.

Brad Thomson had, to my surprise, effortlessly managed to do exactly what Stella had suggested—he had built up a close connection with a female federal cop assigned to the latest sniper shooting, a story referred to in the newsroom by the succinct name "Toddler-Dad."

Brad certainly had superior persuasive powers, as the officer shared with him details of the investigation not only withheld from anyone else in the media, but also far more than professional conduct would dictate. Alec Slater made coarsely jocular remarks about the sexual exploits he imagined Brad had indulged in to gain this level of "fucking pillow talk."

In my persona of Ann Meadows, I gave a very frosty reception to Alec's sniggering comments, but I was very aware that the terms Alec used so jeeringly must be uncomfortably close to Cynthia's opinion of my behavior with Roanna.

I saw Roanna in passing, and each time we greeted each other perfunctorily, as distant acquaintances would. Roanna was often in *The Trump* offices, either discussing the joint advertising campaign/competition featuring Aylmer Island Resort luxury vacations or increasingly with Emmaline Partlow, no doubt for the personal indoctrination into Supremity that Jason Benton had requested as a favor.

The puzzle for me was how close Roanna was to Benton. She'd told ASIO she knew him well from the time he'd spent on Aylmer Island. But how well was *well*? When I'd been undercover at the resort before Jason Benton had been on the scene, I remembered there'd been gossip about Roanna's penchant to break hearts and move on. As far as I could recall, the reference had been exclusively to female hearts, but that didn't entirely rule out the possibility of male lovers.

With an effort, I visualized the distinctly unappealing Benton in bed with the distinctly appealing Roanna. I'd had the same trouble imagining Emmaline Partlow in a clinch with Benton. It wasn't merely that the man was extraordinarily ugly—that was hardly his fault, and this disadvantage could be mitigated by good character and a sweet nature. The problem was Jason Benton combined unfortunate looks with a remarkably unpleasant personality. Surely even his wealth and influence would not be enough to overcome this double whammy, although, when I thought about it, money and power did seem to be an effective antidote to what would otherwise be irredeemably repulsive qualities.

If it became necessary in the future, I thought with a mental shudder, I might have to force myself to flirt with Jason Benton. My skin crawled at the abstract concept, so what would it be like in actuality? It didn't bear thinking about.

One person I had actively decided to court in a restrained Ann Meadows way was Stella Rohm. As deputy managing editor and leader of the Righteous Scourge team, she had access to all levels of the organization, including Benton. Stella also seemed very well-informed on the topic of Supremity and was critical of its leader. Her dislike of Emmaline could be useful, as she no doubt had specific reasons to justify her attitude.

My first step was to join Stella and Lorna Gosling at the gym very early on Thursday morning, having mentioned to Lorna the day before that her quest for physical fitness had been an inspiration for me.

"Really?" she'd cried, enthused. "Just the way Stella's been an inspiration for me!"

"Something like that," I'd said.

Actually, it was pleasure to get back into an exercise routine—I'd been losing my edge while studying for this undercover role. I trotted into the 24-hour gymnasium where we were to meet, allowing myself plenty of leeway so I could pay for a session and then give the place a once-over. I automatically did this with every new environment, checking out the floor plan and establishing where the exits were. In an emergency, I wouldn't waste time trying to find the best escape route—I'd already have it in my head.

My exercise partners arrived together, Lorna gushing, Stella impassive. Both wore expensive, brightly-colored gym outfits in contrast to my plain blue shorts and oversize white T-shirt.

Stella flicked a glance over me. "Good legs," she said.

I flicked a look right back. Was that a sexual comment? Would Ann notice it, if it were? "Thank you," I said modestly.

After we warmed up, we began a program of circuit training Stella had apparently devised.

"How do you keep yourself in such great shape?" gasped Lorna, struggling gamely at the rowing machine next to me.

"I can only put it down to genetics," I declared. I smiled inwardly as I added in a serious tone, "That, and clean, decent living."

Stella, rowing easily at maximum resistance on my other side, gave a short laugh. "Clean living?" she said dryly. "That must be it."

I was pleased to find Stella had a sense of humor—it rather made up for Lorna who was distressingly lacking in that area. Irritatingly, I had to censor any humorous ripostes that occurred to me, because Ann Meadows was a serious, practical woman with very little subtlety to her character. And, I reminded myself severely, she was in mourning, full of sad memories of her husband's illness and death.

In reality, I was rather somber myself. Each evening, when I got home to my flat, I made two phone calls. The first was to Pam to ask about my brother's condition. It was heartening to learn Martin was showing slow but steady improvement and was breathing on his own, although he was still unconscious. The second call was to Cynthia to give my daily report.

Cynthia's manner was friendly, but not too close. After admitting her personal feelings had got in the way, she'd said, "We have a lot to talk about, but only after this assignment is over. Until then . . ."

"Business as usual, Courtney?"

"Business as usual, Ann."

I kept my side of the bargain, but it was difficult to maintain an impersonal front. I felt myself wanting to reach out to someone—to Cynthia—in a way I couldn't remember ever desiring before.

Perhaps this was because Ann was less talkative than me, except when she launched into lecture mode, so I was finding I had more time to reflect. Prior to this, I'd eagerly embraced the present and ignored unsettling memories from the past. Part of the reason I'd decided to go into undercover work was, I now realized, because it gave me the freedom of leaving Denise Cleever behind and submerging myself in someone else's life.

After all this musing, I had to smile. I was indulging in pop psychology. The reason I'd chosen to go undercover was probably more mundane, simply a craving for the excitement that came with playing a high stakes game.

Unless out on assignment, every morning Stella and the members of the team gathered together to review the Righteous Scourge Web site. There were always amendments and additions, usually providing more details of attacks that had already occurred, or deliberately vague, disturbing warnings of attacks yet to come.

After the Thursday early morning workout at the gym, I went home to shower before going to *The Trump*—Ann was the modest type who'd not be comfortable undressing in front of other women. This meant I was last in the room, and the Web site was already up. I saw with quickening interest that the praise for the efficacy of the Toddler-Dad Murders, which had appeared on the site almost as soon as the crime had occurred, now included a very distressing extreme close-up of the toddler's head, showing clearly how the sniper's shot had devastated his little skull.

"Who could have taken that photo?" I asked.

Stella turned to glance at me. "I had the same thought, but it's not one of *The Trump's*. Photographs are filed digitally, so it was easy to check."

"Freelance?" said Jon. "They're getting a lot of money for sniper photos."

"Looks like something taken by the cops' crime scene photographer," said Francesca, who was wearing a very tight pink dress with a scoop neckline to show her cleavage. She tilted her head to regard the page from a different angle. "Is it even at the crime scene?" she said. "Maybe taken at the morgue?"

"What about the Feds? They were there, quick smart, with their own technicians," said Brad.

Leering, Alec asked Brad, "Why don't you check with your little federal bedmate? Or is it all over, lover boy? You pumping fresh meat?"

"Oh, *please*," I said.

Alec switched his leer to me. "What's the matter, Ann? I've offended your delicate sensibilities, have I?"

"Actually, you have," I said, lifting my chin. "Not that it would make any difference to you."

"Let's keep to the matter at hand," Stella said, not hiding her impatience. "It's an excellent idea to check with your contact, Brad. Like Jon says, it's probably a freelancer who's put it up for sale on one of a thousand Web sites."

"If Righteous Scourge purchased the photo that way, it's a potential lead to them," I said.

Stella looked thoughtful. "I guess the intelligence agencies will be on it already."

"The Righteous site is constantly monitored," I said, "so I'm sure they will be." To prove what a helpful addition to the team I was, I added, "I'll check my contacts anyway and see if I can get something you can quote."

Francesca, who was working on an in-depth analysis of terrorists' Web sites with the concentration on Righteous Scourge, said to Stella, "I want it if she gets anything. Tell her to get it straight to me. I can use it." Francesca rarely used my name, in fact, she rarely spoke to me.

"Ann," I said. "The name's Ann, Francesca. Ann."

She rolled her eyes. "Got a self esteem problem, have we?"

"Oh, for God's sake! This isn't children's hour." Stella glared at both of us. "Grow up, you two."

"Naughty, naughty," said Alec grinning. "You girls are just so emotional. I like that in a woman."

I contemplated what a straight-arm jolt to the point of his chin would do. Picturing the result quite calmed me, so I could say with dignity, while sending a pointed look at Francesca, "I like to get on with everybody."

Francesca rolled her eyes again.

The meeting broke up after Stella had asked for brief reports on each person's current assignment. She caught my elbow as I was about to exit the room.

"Warwick Wallace would like to see you."

"Now?"

"He said as soon as possible."

I'd never set eyes on Warwick Wallace before, but in his photographs he gave the impression of being the comfortable avuncular type. He was *The Trump's* managing editor—news, and Stella Rohm's direct superior. He'd been in the States for the last couple of weeks, appearing as a witness in a case for damages brought against his former employer. Wallace was an American, and his file noted that his marriage, already shaky, had broken up when he'd accepted the editor's position in Australia without bothering to consult his wife on the decision.

I knocked on his office door, and entered when commanded to do so. It wasn't a luxurious room, but comfortably furnished and rather untidy.

"I'm Ann Meadows," I said. "You wanted to see me, Mr. Wallace?"

"Warwick, please." He had a faintly twangy American accent.

I nodded politely and waited with fingers linked while he came out from behind his desk and cleared a pile of papers off a chair for me. He was a large man with disproportionately small hands and feet. He had a totally unremarkable face, but shrewd, knowing eyes.

Wheezing a little—his file noted Wallace was an asthmatic—he cleared another chair of papers and positioned it directly in front of me.

Sitting down, he leaned forward to put his elbows on his knees and said, "What are your politics, Ann?"

Although by leaning forward he'd invaded my personal space, I ignored the fact he was too close to me and inclined towards him until our noses were almost touching.

He straightened up in his chair. Round one to Ann Meadows. "My politics?" I frowned. "Why would that be of any interest?"

"Everything about you is of interest to me. I pride myself in being cognizant of the smallest detail where my staff is concerned. Paula assures me you have excellent credentials, but I've read your personnel file, and it's all but bare of anything of substance."

"It was sufficient for Paula Valentine, and she is the editor of *The Austral Trumpeter*," I pointed out with offended dignity. "Moreover, Mr. Wallace, I believe Jason Benton is quite happy to have me in his employ."

Warwick Wallace had reddened slightly, clearly annoyed with me pulling rank on him. "That's as may be," he said, "but you are my responsibility. I'll thank you to answer some questions about your experience and your suitability for the position you have."

I was puzzled by Wallace's attitude. If his superiors had accepted me, why was he making waves? I mentally reviewed what I knew of him. With a solid work record in publishing both magazines and newspapers in the States, he was an unexceptional but very competent middle manager.

"I'm afraid I can give you very little direct information," I said. "As you are no doubt aware, I am legally bound not to reveal anything covered by the various provisions imposed on the intelligence community."

I smiled to myself at this excessively vague statement. I smiled in earnest when he said, "That's ridiculously vague."

"It is," I agreed.

He stretched to take a folder from his desk. "I've a list of questions for you."

I folded my hands in my lap. "I'll answer them as fully as possible, of course, but I suspect there will be severe restrictions on what I am able to say."

"We can start with your politics. What party do you support?"

"From the legal point of view, that is a question you're not entitled to ask. Besides, it can have absolutely no bearing on my job here."

"Of course it has a bearing. Your political beliefs may slant the way you present information."

"What are *your* political leanings, Warwick?" When he glared at me, I said, "It's a very personal thing, and not a question one wants to answer, is it?"

"So, Ann, you're not inclined to cooperate?"

I said nothing. After a moment he got up and slapped the folder down on his desk. With the beginning of a reluctant smile, he said, "Well, Ann Meadows, that was a total waste of time, wasn't it?"

I lifted my shoulders in a slight, polite shrug.

He went over and opened the door for me. As I passed by him, he said, "I'll be watching you."

When I returned to my cubicle I called Tony Scott, my fictional contact at ASIO, about the toddler's photograph. "I'll get back to you," she said. Tony was a woman this morning.

Jon Hong appeared as I was replacing the receiver. "Media release from Rafe Thorne," he said, handing me a printed page. "Stella told me to cover it. Is there an intelligence angle I can use?"

This would be Nancy Otega's work. It was much more elaborate than most media releases. A color photograph of the politician stared out at the reader—his jaw resolutely set, his direct, blue-eyed gaze serious. Underneath were the words: NATIONAL SECURITY A GRASSROOTS ISSUE! YOUR COMMUNITY NEEDS YOU!

The release went on to state that because of the incompetence of the government at all levels, the people of Australia had become cannon fodder for vicious terrorist groups. Citizens died while the politicians ate cake. The intelligence bodies, beholden as they were to the administration, were hamstrung in their efforts to destroy Righteous Scourge and end the funding of attacks.

It was time for Aussies to take charge. Today, Rafe Thorne was announcing that some weeks ago he had initiated the formation of Terrorist Watch to protect the men, women and children in the district he had the honor to represent in Parliament. Funded entirely by Right Way, and headed by experts in the field, Terrorist Watch would mobilize citizens to mount continuous surveillance of their own neighborhoods, to be ever vigilant and proactive, so that terrorists would be detected before they could carry out their deadly missions.

Thorne ended the media release with the plea that other politicians, whatever their party affiliations, would join with Right Way in this citizen-based, grassroots campaign and establish similar Terrorist Watch organizations in their own districts.

"I don't believe ASIO and the like are going to be happy to be described as *hamstrung*," I observed. With a grin I added, "How about I get you a quote from what's grandly called *an informed source*? Could you use that?"

"Perfect," Jon said with a smile. "And can the informed source be discreetly livid? It makes for more conflict that way."

"I think I can manage that," I said, thinking how clever Rafe Thorne had been to describe the intelligence community as *hamstrung* rather than accusing them of being bungling and inept. That way he didn't make enemies of those who might impede his rise to power.

My phone rang. It was Tony Scott. "As you know, everything that appears on that particular site is scrutinized as a matter of course. Nothing so far on the photo, but it's an interesting question. I'll get back to you if we turn anything up."

"Rafe Thorne's just put out a media release describing intelligence services as hamstrung in their efforts to defeat terrorism," I said. "Now, Tony, how does that make you feel? Bitter? Angry?"

She laughed. "Hamstrung?" she said. "That sounds pretty accurate to me!"

CHAPTER THIRTEEN

Emmaline's limousine was a gleaming black Lincoln Town Car imported from the States. The steering wheel had not been converted to the right side and the vehicle alerted drivers with a sign on the back that read CAUTION: LEFT-HAND DRIVE.

When the limousine arrived at my flat on Saturday morning, Kenny, still wearing what looked like the same dark suit, got out to take my overnight bag and open the passenger door for me. Along with his bodyguard duties, he obviously doubled as chauffeur.

As I stepped into the cavernous back of the limo and sank into a soft, leather seat, Emmaline greeted me with enthusiasm. Her stocky body was clad in deep purple pants and a paler purple tunic. I thought her silver pageboy hair had a hint of mauve in it, but decided it was probably a reflection from her clothing.

I looked down at my own boring outfit. Ann certainly didn't wear jeans, so I had chosen tailored tan slacks and a cream blouse. Naturally on my feet I had neat leather walking shoes, not sneakers.

"I'm looking forward to seeing Supremity Sanctuary," I said, ever the dutiful guest.

"I can promise you experiences you've never had before."

Apparently she wasn't promising sexual delights—at least, I didn't think so. "What sort of experiences?" I asked, a cautious note in my voice.

"At Supremity Sanctuary you will go through one of those life-changing events that occur only occasionally in one's existence. It will open your eyes to vistas you've never dreamed of before."

"I'm sure the weekend will be very interesting."

Emmaline fixed me with her dark, magnetic eyes. "Interesting? No! Life changing! Life affirming!"

Kenny, who'd been stowing my overnight bag in the boot, checked that the passenger door was shut properly, then got into the driver's seat. With a purr, the limousine took off smoothly. "Not just a bodyguard, your driver, too," I observed.

"It's part of his duties. Naturally, Kenny has been through an exhaustive driving course to prepare for any eventuality. Should we be attacked, he will know exactly what evasive strategies to use."

Looking surprised, I said, "Do you really believe you're in danger?"

"I've received threats," she said darkly.

I revved my surprise up another notch. "Threats? Credible threats?"

She grimaced. "Several in revolting detail. Torture and then a slow death."

"That suggests kidnapping first, so you can be moved to a secure location before any torture is inflicted."

Emmaline looked quite startled at my matter-of-fact tone. "That's why I have Kenny," she said. "He's here to make sure nothing like that can ever happen."

"What do the police say?"

She jutted her heavy jaw. "I haven't contacted the authorities. They won't take me seriously, if I do."

"I'm sure they will." I assumed a professional demeanor to add, "Emmaline, my career in intelligence has taught me the importance of taking threats seriously."

"I'm handling it." Her tone suggested the discussion was over.

In the silence that followed, I examined the interior of the limousine. The windows were heavily tinted so no one could look in. Leather and chrome were everywhere. A minibar was stocked with various alcoholic beverages and a wide range of juices and soft drinks. A chrome flask held coffee. Packaged snacks were available. A flat screen TV, blank at the moment, was angled for viewing. Soft music played.

I was deciding I could become accustomed to this life when Emmaline broke into my thoughts. "You've met Warwick Wallace."

"I have."

"What did you think of him?"

"He asked me a lot of questions."

Amused, Emmaline said, "Did you answer them?"

"Not really."

"Warwick's spoken to me about you."

I raised my eyebrows. "He has? If Mr. Wallace had a problem with me, I would have thought he'd approach Paula Valentine. She's the editor."

"Warwick Wallace and I go back a long way."

"Do you?" This was interesting, as this connection hadn't been in any files I'd reviewed. "How is that?"

She made a vague gesture. "You bump into people as time goes by. Sometimes, for no apparent reason, they enter your life again and again."

"I imagine Supremity teaches you that these are not simple coincidences."

Emmaline narrowed her eyes. "I hadn't realized you'd studied *The Supremity Chronicles*, Ann."

"I haven't, at least not yet. I've gone to the gym a couple of times this week with Lorna and Stella. Lorna's very keen to tell me about Supremity, and she's mentioned meaningful coincidences several times."

The idea of meaningful coincidences was a direct steal from the theory of synchronicity. It was clear that to build Supremity's scriptural basis, Emmaline had been a magpie, collecting a hodgepodge of concepts and ideas from various religious and philosophical movements including pop psychology and the loonier fringes of New Age.

"I've arranged for you to have your own, special deluxe copy of *The Supremity Chronicles*," Emmaline said, "autographed by myself."

I murmured appreciatively, hoping she wasn't going to test me on the contents of her scriptures. I had an uneasy feeling she would expect, at the least, memorization of the basic tenets of her half-baked religion.

With one of her abrupt change of subjects, Emmaline said, "Politics."

I put on a puzzled frown. "Yes?"

"Warwick asked you about your politics."

Looking vexed, I said, "Mr. Wallace had no right to ask. It's a very personal matter, as I told him."

"*I'm* asking." Her emphatic tone was meant to intimidate.

Obediently, I looked unsettled. "Essentially, I'm apolitical," I said. "My career was in national security, and over the years I've served under several administrations. I always thought it best to avoid a strong political stance."

"So you were wishy-washy?"

I couldn't prevent a smile. "If you like to put it that way, Emmaline, I'd say yes, I was."

Gazing intently at me, she said, "Now you're free of your self-imposed obligation to be even-handed, what's your opinion of the present administration?"

"Weak, hopeless, vacillating . . ." I paused to consider. It was important I said what Emmaline wanted to hear. "The prime minister and his cabinet seem incapable of coping with the challenge of these indiscriminate terrorist killings. We desperately need a strong leader, willing to take whatever steps, however draconian, to save our country before career politicians bring Australia to its knees."

She smiled at me approvingly. "Excellent," she said. "Just what I hoped to hear."

Because of recent rain, the countryside approaching the site of Supremity Sanctuary—insiders called it the Esses—was particularly green and lush. Even the gray-green leaves of the gum trees were clean and glistened in the sunlight.

I'd seen a floor plan of the complex, but had no concept of what it looked like in reality. I was expecting something ostentatious, sticking out like a sore thumb in all this natural beauty, so I was pleasantly surprised when Kenny drove through the entrance gates, to see how the buildings blended in with the landscape.

"Environmentally sound design," said Emmaline. "From the rooftop to the foundations, everything is ecologically sound. We have solar panels backed up by generators, our own water supply—in the event of a disaster we would be self-sufficient for some time."

We were met at the door by Lorna, back in her uniform of white tunic and sandals, her lank brown hair tied back with a golden ribbon. She beamed up at me. "You're going to *love* it here!"

Inside, the surprises continued. I had expected extravagant luxury, but the decor continued the unassuming character of the exterior. The predominant colors were white and pale gold. The furniture was simple and functional.

"No shades of purple?" I said to Emmaline.

She looked at me sternly. "All tones of purple throw out protective vibrations to negate the power of those who are spiritually poisonous. Such vibrations are not needed here. You must understand, Ann, that this is the hub, the very core of Supremity in the southern hemisphere. Thus it is a place of enlightenment, not impinged upon by the dark forces of the world. The colors of white and gold symbolize the fully actualized spirit, the zenith for which we all strive."

Kenny turned up with our bags. Emmaline's was a lavender custom-made Louis Vuitton, mine a mass-produced black vinyl.

"Kenny, take my bag to my suite. I'll follow in a moment." Emmaline turned to me. "Lorna will give you a tour of the Esses. I'd do so myself, but I'm afraid I have pressing matters to attend to."

"Rafe Thorne's arrived," said Lorna. "He's in the Sphere."

"Excellent." After dismissing me with a regal inclination of her head, she hurried off after Kenny.

So the rising political star was to be here for the weekend. I wondered who else was invited. I pictured his tiny, blond PR dynamo. "Did Nancy Otega come with Rafe?"

Lorna gave a contemptuous snort. "She couldn't if she wanted to, because Emmaline refuses to let her enter the Esses.

Nancy has a sick, sick soul." She leaned towards me to say confidentially, "Just between us, I don't think she'll be working for Rafe much longer."

"That's a bit of a shock," I said. "At the dinner party the other night, Nancy spoke to me most positively about Emmaline."

"Oh, Nancy admires Emmaline for all the help she's given Rafe and Right Way. But like I told you before, Nancy's an enemy of our faith. Did you know she actually called us a noxious cult? Would you believe that!"

I shook my head. "Most unpleasant."

Lorna picked up my bag. "I'll take you to your accommodation. Emmaline has put you in a lodge."

From her tone, this was quite an honor. "This is a good thing?" I asked.

"Oh, yes. Only special guests have lodges."

Why was I so special? A warning sounded in my head. This couldn't be a trap, could it? To get me away in the country in a cult compound where no one could help me? But what would that achieve? I grinned to myself. Perhaps Emmaline aimed to break my resistance by forcing me to listen to *The Supremity Chronicles* read aloud by the author from beginning to end.

The lodge was one of several small cabins built into a low hillside. It was a lovely setting, with a small stream gurgling happily nearby. Each lodge had a veranda at the front. Inside it was quite lovely, with wooden walls and comfortable furnishings. There was one main room dominated by a wide fireplace. The furniture was simple—a king-size bed, bedside table, a main table with chairs and a long sofa in front of the fireplace. Off this central room was a tiny kitchen and a well-appointed bathroom.

Ann wouldn't gush, so I said, "This is very nice."

Lorna pointed to an adjacent lodge. "That's where Rafe Thorne is staying."

"He seems destined for greatness," I remarked.

Lorna took the bait. "Emmaline says he'll be prime minister one day."

"Really? But the prime minister is the leader of the party with the majority of seats. There are only two major parties, and Rafe Thorne doesn't belong to either of them, so how can that be?"

She looked mysterious. "I can't say."

"But you know?" I said admiringly.

Shaking her head, Lorna put her finger to her lips. No way was she going to make it easy for me.

"You were going to show me around . . ."

"Of course. Follow me."

We passed another lodge, and a woman came out onto the veranda. "Hi," she said. It was Stella Rohm. She'd said she'd be at the Esses, so I wasn't surprised to see her.

I gave her a sedate wave. "Hello."

When we were further down the hill, Lorna said, "I suppose you're asking yourself why Stella is in a lodge. Like, she usually stays in the staff quarters."

"So why is she in a lodge?"

"It's so exciting. Stella's decided to agree to be initiated into Supremity!"

"Really? I had no idea—"

"Emmaline is so pleased!" She clasped her hands. "I think I can take a little bit of credit for Stella's decision. She's a searcher of truth, and I've taken the opportunity to talk to her about Supremity during our mornings at the gym."

"That's nice," I said, wondering why it was that Stella, who had made it plain she didn't believe in Supremity and was only playing along for the good of her career, would go this far. Maybe she had a hidden agenda, like me.

CHAPTER FOURTEEN

Lorna was clearly accustomed to escorting visitors around the Esses. She kept up a running tour-guide commentary as we walked around the complex. It was larger than it appeared. Where possible, buildings had been designed to complement the contours of the land, and all, Lorna assured me, had at least one floor underground.

The staff quarters she'd referred to earlier were housed in a two-story block not far from the main building. "I suppose you have quite a staff to run this place," I said. "Does everyone working here belong to Supremity?"

"Why, of course. This is the Sanctuary. People who don't follow Emmaline's teachings have auras that are contaminated, and would disturb the higher vibrations."

Her solemn acceptance of all this had me fighting to keep a smile at bay. I said gravely, "What about visitors? Me, for example. At our first meeting Emmaline told me my aura was rather suspect, I'm afraid."

"There is a cleansing ritual after visitors leave," said Lorna reassuringly, "so you mustn't worry yourself about disturbing the vibrations. Besides, Emmaline would not allow anyone into the Esses whose aura was badly diseased. That's why Nancy Otega isn't welcome."

She patted my arm consolingly. "Anyway, I'm sure yours has improved a great deal since you first met Emmaline. She radiates light, you know, although it's invisible to the ordinary person."

"I see. Well, actually, I don't see"—it was impossible to suppress a giggle—"if you see what I mean."

Get serious, Denise!

"I'm sorry," I said. "I'm a bit overwhelmed by all this."

Lorna nodded solemnly. "People often are."

Several people were using the deluxe facilities in the Fitness Axis, which housed the gymnasium, swimming pool and spa that Stella had mentioned.

"Has Emmaline told you about the importance of a healthy body—"

"She has, Lorna. She has." I had no compunction in interrupting her, because there was no way I was up for a repeat of the mind-numbing lecture Emmaline had delivered on the subject of fit minds in fit bodies.

Next to the Fitness Axis was the Mediaplex, where original programs and training materials were created.

My tour of the Esses ended at the central building. Beside it was a landscaped area with white tables and chairs arranged in a circle. "This is where we're having a barbecue tonight to welcome guests to the Esses."

She gestured towards the main structure and said reverently, "And this is the focal point, the heart of Supremity Sanctuary."

I'd only seen the entrance hall when I'd arrived, but now Lorna took me through the rest of the building, with the exception of the private suites upstairs, reserved for Emmaline and others of high position in the movement.

There were administrative offices, and a series of meeting rooms of various sizes, some furnished conventionally, others piled with cushions for informal gatherings. A well-appointed auditorium was available for large numbers. In the huge state-of-the-art kitchen, the staff, all wearing the requisite white tunics and sandals, was busy preparing lunch. My stomach growled. It had been a long time since breakfast, and I regretted not eating something in the limousine.

"This is the center of the building," Lorna said, halting outside gleaming white double doors, beautifully inlaid with a pattern of golden S shapes. "The Sphere," she said in a hushed tone. She dropped her voice to a whisper to add, "We can peek in, but you must be very quiet."

"I will be," I whispered back.

As befitted its name, the Sphere's walls and ceiling—white with ribs of gold—formed a continuous surface in the shape of a globe. We ventured inside onto the white marble floor. It was like standing in half a tennis ball. Light speared down from a skylight situated at the apex of the globe, illuminating like a spotlight the only furniture in the space, an ornate golden chair placed in the very center of the floor. Rafe Thorne sat there in white robes, his hands linked together on his lap, his eyes shut.

Quite unnecessarily, Lorna took my arm and breathed, "Shhh." Then she pointed back at the doors through which we'd just entered. I nodded, and we beat an almost silent retreat.

After the doors had closed on Thorne, I said, "What is he doing? Meditating?"

"Finding the still point of his inner self," said Lorna. "I can't say more unless you're initiated."

As we walked back the way we'd come, I said, wrinkling my forehead with concern, "That's not supposed to happen this weekend, is it? To me? I mean, I'm intrigued by Supremity, but—"

I broke off as Lorna literally went off into peals of laughter. I didn't smile, but stood on my dignity. At last she spluttered, "The preparation is awfully demanding and you haven't even read *The Chronicles* yet. Besides, you can't just decide to join Supremity. You have to be gathered."

"I'm glad that I amuse you," I announced in a hurt tone.

Immediately contrite, Lorna said, "I'm sorry, Ann. I didn't mean to laugh at you. Forgive me. But there is a lot of preparation before you make the decision to accept initiation."

"Has Stella Rohm done all this demanding preparation?"

"Stella is doing the accelerated mode. Emmaline has found her spirit particularly evolved."

"So there are shortcuts?" I said. "You didn't mention that before."

Lorna looked at me kindly. "Unfortunately, Ann, your aura, as you said yourself, has imperfections. That means the accelerated mode is not suitable for you."

"I'll have to work on cleansing my aura," I said with what I thought was admirable determination.

Lorna checked her watch. "You're scheduled for 'Through Grief to Joy' at two. We've just got time for a quick lunch."

The large dining hall had been set up for a buffet lunch of cold meats and various salads. Instead of the ubiquitous color scheme of white and gold, the walls and ceiling were a pale green, and the tables and chairs a slightly deeper green. When I commented on this to Lorna, she said Emmaline herself had chosen the shades to promote calm digestion.

"So Emmaline's involved in every aspect," I remarked.

Lorna spread her hands. "Without her, there would be nothing," she said with simple sincerity.

I piled a plate indelicately high and joined Lorna at a table. The dining hall was rapidly filling, and the hum of conversation was growing louder. I saw Kenny come in alone. Watching his slow, deliberate pace, I was reminded of an inexorable force. In some subtle way, he was full of menace.

"In the car this morning," I said to Lorna, "Emmaline mentioned she'd received threats."

She nodded soberly. "Emmaline says you must strike first. She calls it anticipatory defense."

"She didn't mention that. What does it actually mean?"

Lorna put down her fork, and gave me a long, considered look. "You'll have to ask Emmaline," she said. "It's part of Supremity's inner doctrine. I've already said too much, just mentioning it."

By the time we left the dining hall, almost every seat was taken. "Are all these people members of Supremity?" I asked.

"Many are seekers, looking for meaning in their lives." Lorna was very earnest. "They're selected by gatherers to come to the Esses for clarity sessions, where they explore who they are and why they've been put on this earth."

"Will I be doing a clarity session?"

"I have you scheduled for one tomorrow morning, after your aura cleansing. Right now, you need to be in your grief session. I'll take you there."

As we were leaving the main building, a car pulled up. Paula Valentine got out one side, a man out the other. She said something to him, then swept past us with a regal nod, and disappeared inside.

The man opened the boot of the car and started unloading their luggage.

"That's Paula's husband," said Lorna. "Isn't he a hunk?"

Lorna calling someone a hunk? I stared at her, then I stared at him. She was right—he was. Paula Valentine's third husband had a good body, he wore his very expensive country-squire clothes with élan, and his face, though far from classically handsome, was compelling. He had deep blue eyes and a strong chin with a dimple. As he saw Lorna, he flashed excellent teeth in a smile that attractively crinkled the corners of his eyes.

Her gaze fixed on him, she said, "He's going into politics. Isn't that great? Someone like Mitchell Nash is just who this country needs."

"He's joining Rafe Thorne's party?"

She tore her eyes away from Mitchell Nash to give me a look of mild astonishment. "Of *course* Rafe's Right Way party. What else?"

Lorna delivered me to a tall, soft-spoken man dressed in a long white robe. He introduced himself as Keiran and took me through a gateway into the precise order of a peaceful Japanese garden. We sat together on a stone bench beside a gorgeous pool of koi fish saying nothing. I'd mentally rehearsed all the details of my widowhood and was ready to emote in a refined way, but Keiran didn't give me the opportunity.

"Let the beauty flow into you," he said at last. "Allow thoughts to rise without your will, like fish drawn to the silver surface of the water."

Another long silence. I could hear the faint buzz of insects, the ripple of water, the muted chatter of some little bird. My wary impatience began to leak away. Unbidden, an image of Martin, lying immobile in his hospital bed, came into my mind. I felt tears prick my eyelids.

Keiran said gently, "Allow your thoughts to float like leaves in an ever-flowing stream. Let your pain, your grief, your anger be washed away with them."

We sat together for a long, long time. With nothing to distract me, memories ran like a continuous, fragmented movie on an inner screen—hurtful things I'd forgotten, moments of delight submerged by time, snatches of conversation . . .

"Through grief to joy."

Keiran's words brought me back to the Japanese garden. I found my cheeks wet with tears.

"What do you feel?" he said.

"Release."

He nodded and got slowly to his feet. "Stay here as long as you need."

I sat there alone until the sound of wind chimes roused me.

When I made my way back to my lodge, *The Supremity Chronicles* was on the table, waiting for me. I consciously shook off the extraordinary experience I'd just had and before examining the book, did a quick search of the lodge to check for listening devices. I wouldn't detect anything really advanced, but fortunately most people relied on commercially available equipment, which was harder to conceal.

Finding nothing, I sat down to examine *The Chronicles*. This volume was not the gold leather and pretend-parchment book I'd skimmed through as part of my preparation, but a gorgeous object, obviously handmade and very costly. The cover appeared to be ivory—I frowned, hoping it had been harvested before the ban—with the title and author engraved into the surface and filled with gold. Under the title on the front appeared: WRITTEN BY THE INSPIRED HAND OF EMMALINE PARTLOW IMPARTING THE HOLY WORDS OF AN ULTIMATE BEING.

Inside, Emmaline's flamboyant signature on the title page was—no surprise—in purple ink.

The scriptures were printed on genuine parchment, and I was examining the heavy pages when I was startled by a sharp knock on the front door. I'd noticed earlier there wasn't a lock, just a latch, so I didn't get up from the table, but called out, "Come in."

"Getting comfortable?" said Stella Rohm. I couldn't help noticing how her snugly fitting jeans and skimpy top emphasized her excellent body. She'd recently been swimming or had a shower as her short, blond hair was wet and slicked back behind her ears.

I indicated a seat, then hefted *The Chronicles*. Reminding myself I was Ann Meadows—for some reason I found it harder to play the part in Stella Rohm's company—I said in a serious tone, "I'm wondering if there's anything in Supremity for me."

"I wouldn't think so. You're not credulous enough."

"And you are? From what you said back in Sydney, Stella, I had no idea you had any ambitions to be inducted into the Supremity family."

Amused, she said, "Did Lorna tell you Emmaline has me on a fast track?"

"She said something about an accelerated mode. Have you changed your mind and decided to join?"

"Let's say I'm considering my options." With a cynical smile, Stella leaned forward to put her elbows on the table. "What do you really make of all this, Ann? To me, you don't seem to be the type to be sucked in by a pseudo-religion."

"I don't know if it is a pseudo-religion," I protested mildly.

"It is," Stella said with conviction.

"Then why are you joining it?"

"I'm playing the same game as you are."

"Game? I don't know what you mean."

She grinned. "I think you do, Ann. I think you do."

A knock on the door gave me a welcome moment to marshal my thoughts. The white tunic and sandals marked the slight young man as a Supremity staff member.

"Sorry to interrupt," he said. Looking past me he saw Stella seated at the table. "Oh, good. I've left a message on your lodge's door, but now I can deliver it in person. Emmaline is inviting you both to cocktails in her private rooms before the barbecue. She'll expect you in half an hour. Dress is informal— come as you are."

"I'll change anyway," said Stella, after he'd gone. "Emmaline doesn't altogether approve of jeans."

Pausing at the door, she turned to say, "We must continue our conversation later. It was just getting interesting."

My earlier calm gained from my time in the Japanese garden had disappeared. I paced restlessly around the lodge. What in the hell was Stella up to? And what did she suspect about Ann Meadows that made her secure in speaking so slightingly of Supremity? Surely Stella's position with *The Trump* would be in jeopardy if I were to repeat what she'd said to Emmaline.

Suddenly I hungered for the sound of Cynthia's voice. I wished I could call and get her take on this development. I couldn't use my cell phone—such transmissions were very risky, and I wouldn't trust any phone here at the Sanctuary. Speaking with Cynthia was out of the question, unless some emergency situation arose.

And this wasn't an emergency—yet.

CHAPTER FIFTEEN

I wasn't sure if Stella expected that we'd walk over to the main building together, but if so, she was in for a disappointment. I suspected my next private conversation with her would be a critical one, so I wanted time to think things through.

After freshening up and changing my cream blouse for a blue silk shirt, I set off at a brisk walk. The Esses really had a delightful setting, and the slowly darkening air was cool against my face. I thought back to the session in the garden, trying to see it through my normally skeptical eyes. What had happened, after all? Not much. I'd sat on a bench next to a soft-spoken man, who had murmured a few platitudes. I'd had a moment of weakness and let myself become maudlin over things in the past I couldn't change.

That was the cool, rational explanation. I hardly let myself admit that there had been more to the experience than that. If only I could capture that feeling of release, of peace again . . . I gave myself a mental shake. This place was getting to me.

Muted luxury characterized Emmaline's private suite. The cocktails were served in a room with a pristine white carpet. The comfortably plush sofas and chairs were upholstered in deliciously buttery yellow. Behind the white and gold bar stood Kenny—clearly a man of all trades, including bartending.

I hesitated at the door, half expecting to see Roanna, and actively hoping that I wouldn't. There'd been no hint that she would be at The Esses this weekend, but I was braced to deal with it if she was.

I frowned to myself. Why braced? Before this assignment, I would have welcomed the chance to spend some time with her, whether I was playing a role or not. But now I prickled with the uneasy thought that all this time she'd fooled me—she'd fooled everyone.

My apprehension was unnecessary. Roanna wasn't there.

Emmaline, seeing me at the door, sailed over. She was an arresting sight, her thickset body swathed entirely in gold. "Ann, come with me and meet Mitchell Nash. Paula, of course, you know." She beamed at Nash. "He's soon to be a VIP in every sense."

"Thank you, Emmaline, for your confidence."

Close up, Mitchell looked older than my first impression of him. I knew he was in his early thirties, but subtle signs of dissipation were evident on his face. Perhaps it had something to do with the brandy snifter in his hand. He greeted me with a practiced smile, said a few polite words, then tossed off the cognac as though it were water.

"Thirsty business," he said jovially. "Be back in a moment."

Paula watched him head for the bar, her expression frosty. "We'll have to keep an eye on that," Emmaline said to her.

"Yes, we will."

I filed away that Mitchell Nash had a drinking problem. Not a helpful failing for a would-be politician, embarking on a career that would keep him so much in the public eye.

I collected a glass of white wine from Kenny to give me something to hold and then circulated in a diffident way, making small talk and establishing who was there. Warwick Wallace's bulk loomed in a corner where he was in animated conversation with Stella, who'd acknowledged me with an ironic lift of an eyebrow when she'd come into the room.

There was a murmur when consummate politician Rafe Thorne entered, smiling. When I'd seen him in the Sphere he'd been in a white robe, but now he wore a plain gray suit. As a concession to the informality requested, he'd discarded his tie, and his shirt was open at the neck.

He glad-handed his way around the room, stopping at me to say, "Ann, isn't it? We met at Emmaline's dinner party." Smile and never forget a name—the successful pollie's mantra. "I believe we were scheduled to have a little talk. We must do that."

"Nancy not here?" I said, just to see how he'd respond. "I had such a nice conversation with her last Monday night."

He didn't miss a beat. "No, I'm sorry, she's not," he said regretfully. "She couldn't make it."

Thorne left me for bigger fish, and I resumed my slow progress through the room, memorizing faces and, if I could, putting names to them. There were several skeletally thin women wearing tight black dresses to emphasize their dedication to socially-condoned anorexia, and quite a few sleek, well-fed men exuding that sense of privilege that seems to go with indecent wealth.

Very few people sat on the yellow sofas or chairs, preferring to stand in small groups, talking. Individuals would drift to the bar, pick up a refill and drift back to rejoin the animated discussion.

There seemed to be only two topics of conversation, urban terrorism and politics, and these were interrelated. Emmaline and Rafe Thorne were entertaining by far the largest and most spirited group. I joined the edge of it to find out what was going on, noticing Stella standing on the other side.

"In the States," Emmaline was saying, "the vagaries of that dinosaur the Electoral College mean the Republicans and Democrats have the whole thing sewn up. The situation of a third party is hopeless—just ask Ross Perot. We need election reform."

"Ah, but in Australia," said Thorne with a broad grin, "the preferential voting system gives smaller parties some clout. A strong third party has a real chance to influence the government."

"Influence? It's bloody blackmail," someone guffawed. "If you've got enough members in Parliament, you have the majority party by the balls. They have to listen to you and make concessions if they are to get your support for their legislation."

"That's what we need!" exclaimed one of the eating-disorder women. "A strong third party led by Rafe."

This led to general murmurs of assent and some applause. Mitchell Nash handed his glass to his wife, then clapped with particular enthusiasm.

Rafe Thorne put his hand up for silence. "I don't intend to lead a strong third party for long. Right Way will have a majority within two election cycles."

"My God, Rafe! That'll make you prime minister!"

Much laughter and mockery followed this comment. Rafe Thorne smiled through it all, a complacent gleam in his eyes.

"First," he said, "we have to bring the present government down."

"They're tottering now," said a rotund guy with blubbery lips. "I say kick 'em where it hurts."

"It's true that this is no time for half measures," Thorne declared. "The attacks orchestrated by Righteous Scourge have exposed the fatal weakness of our so-called leaders. Another string of attacks with high casualties . . ."

He spread his hands, inviting them to visualize the result.

"The public will be baying for blood," said Emmaline. "And politicians will be running scared. Things will escalate—"

"And we know how to do that!" The rotund guy was at it again.

Emmaline glared at the man who'd dared to interrupt her. "As I was saying, things will escalate, there'll be a vote of no confidence in the prime minister and his cabinet. He'll resign in disgrace, leaving his party in total disarray. Down comes the government. A general election will have to be called."

"Hear, hear," said Mitchell, nodding energetically. He appeared to have taken the role of chief cheerleader.

Warwick Wallace came lumbering over to the group to say, "Breaking news, folks. A shoulder-fired missile's brought down a passenger plane at Sydney Airport."

At the barbecue, the downed plane was the main topic of conversation. Emmaline had arranged for a large flat-screen television to be set up, and most guests, plates in hand, clustered around watching avidly as flames destroyed what was left of the jumbo jet, television journalists indulged in media-speak hysteria and estimates of fatalities scrolled along the bottom of the screen.

Some at the barbecue were plainly horrified, but it was sickening to see the number who saw this tragedy solely in terms of how it would give a boost to Rafe Thorne's campaign.

"The prime minister is toast. Toast!" said one, apparently not realizing the link this allusion had with the fate of the hapless passengers on the plane.

I'd heard enough, so duty didn't require me to stay longer to monitor the crowd's remarks. I selected a steak from those offered to me by a cook, added a baked potato and sour cream, then found a seat at the furthest table from the action, and mercifully alone, moodily ate my meal.

I'd almost finished when Warwick Wallace carefully placed a bottle of red wine and a glass on my table, then, with a wheeze, lowered his heavy body into a chair. "Shocking catastrophe," he said. "Terribly tragic."

"Yes."

As he filled his glass, I noticed again his small, short-fingered hands. He took a gulp, sighed, then said, "But an ill wind, eh? Somebody always benefits."

I wanted to totally level him, but as Ann Meadows, I was constrained. "Perhaps tragedies always happen for a reason," I remarked.

"Not drinking, Ann?" he said, gesturing with the wine bottle. I recognized the label—a fine shiraz from the Clare Valley, South Australia. "Get yourself a glass."

"Thank you, no. I don't particularly like alcohol."

Wallace's chair creaked as he leaned back to regard me with an indulgent smile. "What a straitlaced little woman you are." He chuckled. "Not that it's a bad thing."

"Some of your best friends are straitlaced?"

My sardonic remark was out before I could stop it.

His gaze had sharpened. "Well, well," he said. "A wit, indeed. That's quite a surprise."

I tried to salvage the situation by saying with an irritated frown, "I have standards, Mr. Wallace. Personal standards. If that makes me old-fashioned and dull, then that's too bad. I'm not about to change."

After demolishing another glass of good quality shiraz—totally wasted on the man—Wallace said, "Emmaline tells me you discussed your political beliefs with her. May I point out you refused to do so with me."

I gusted a long-suffering sigh. "I don't know how many times I have to say it's a private matter."

"It's not private if it has to do with your future employment."

A thread of excitement ran through me. Was he going to offer something that would take me a step closer to finding if there were connections among *The Trump* and Supremity and Righteous Scourge?

"What future employment would that be? I must tell you, I'm very happy at *The Trump*."

"The newspaper's a short-term project. What we have in mind is much more interesting. Unfortunately I can't give you details now."

"Why me?" I asked, really meaning the question.

"I've been watching your work closely. Let's just say you have an excellent background in intelligence and have amply demonstrated the breadth of your knowledge."

With more wheezing, he lumbered to his feet. He swayed slightly, and I realized he was drunk. "Emmaline will speak to you tomorrow. Until then, sweet lady"—he raised his glass in a salute—"good night."

I decided to slip away to my room. I located Emmaline holding court near the TV screen and Rafe Thorne, accompanied by Mitchell Nash, still glad-handing from table to table. Politics, I decided, was an exhausting pursuit.

I looked for Stella, but couldn't see her anywhere. Perhaps, like me, she needed to escape this callous bunch.

Nobody noticed me leaving or if they did, it was of no consequence to anyone. Inconspicuous lighting illuminated the pathways with a diffuse light, quite enough to see one's way but not so bright as to wash out the glorious arch of stars in the Milky Way. I halted and tipped my head back to search for the Southern Cross. I remembered that it was Martin who had taught me how to use the constellation to find true south.

Abruptly, I felt trapped. I was caught in this place until tomorrow evening, unable to speak with Cynthia or to find out from Pam how my brother's recovery was progressing. How funny it was that for years I hadn't cared to learn anything about Martin, and now he was constantly in my thoughts.

I strolled along, enjoying the night and the solitude. The steps to my lodge had the same diffuse lighting as the pathways. As I stepped onto the veranda, a shadow moved in the darkness. Automatically, I went to attack mode.

"I wondered how long you'd be," Stella said.

"You nearly frightened me to death!" She didn't know it, but she'd narrowly escaped serious physical harm.

I heard the clink of glasses. "I brought a nightcap with me," she said. "French champagne."

After the day I'd had, champagne sounded good to me. I opened the door, switched on the light. "Come right on in."

The champagne bottle was in a chrome bucket filled with ice. "I do things in style," she said, putting the champagne and two glasses on the table.

"So I see."

I admired the way she opened the bottle without fuss. The cork popped discreetly, the foaming liquid bubbled into the glasses. Stella picked one up and toasted me. "To the night. May it be rewarding."

I frowned at her. "I'm not sure what that means."

She gave me a quick smile. "You'll soon find out."

Could she mean to seduce Ann Meadows? Surely not. We

sat on the sofa companionably. I rarely drank champagne, but tonight the bubbles tickled my palate with a delicious zing. When Stella poured me another glass, I said, "Are you trying to make me tipsy?"

"Absolutely."

I looked at her over the rim of my champagne flute. "Why?"

"I was thinking of staying the night with you."

"Staying? You don't mean—"

"Oh, yes, I do."

I felt a sudden tickle of desire. The champagne talking. Ann Meadows said sternly, "I'm not like that."

Stella gave me a lazy smile. "How do you know until you try?"

My brow creased with bewilderment, I said, "But weren't you married? Don't you have a son?"

"Yes and yes."

I turned my palms up. "Well . . ."

"Ann, just relax. Leave it all to me."

With a frisson of alarm I realized it sounded like a delightful thing to do. Obviously the champagne had gone to my head. "I don't think so. I'm not interested."

She reached out to run a finger down my bare arm. Goose bumps rose. Stella gave a low chuckle. "See, you do like it."

"I don't."

"Your body does."

I crossed my arms protectively over my chest. "I wouldn't know what to do."

"Just put yourself in my hands. I promise you, you'll enjoy the experience."

I had a suspicion she was right. I said firmly, "I'd like for you to leave now."

She grinned. "You don't mean that."

"I do mean it."

A wicked, carnal voice whispered in my ear, *Pillow talk. When her guard is down, who knows what she will say?*

She leaned forward to kiss my throat. It was all I could do not to incline towards her. "Please," I protested.

"Your heart's racing."

"I'm alarmed. Who wouldn't be?"

Stella dropped her hand from my shoulder to my breast. "I don't see you running away."

"I'm not, but I should . . ." My voice trailed off in a long sigh.

How ironic was this? Stella seducing me to lower my defenses and find out what I was up to and me playing reluctant seducee with exactly the same thing in mind.

CHAPTER SIXTEEN

Candidates for the aura purification protocol had to consume a special breakfast, a disgustingly healthy repast of cereals, nuts and fruit. No coffee or tea, just plain water. The sanitization of my subpar aura was to be carried out in the Sphere. I was one of fifteen subjects—eight women and seven men—apparently in need of decontamination.

Adjacent to the Sphere were male and female locker rooms where we all changed into pure white garments rather like gigantic T-shirts and then padded, barefoot, into the center of the marble floor to form a respectful semicircle around Emmaline who, white-robed, was seated in the golden chair I'd seen Rafe Thorne in the day before. On either side of her stood an attendant.

Emmaline rambled on at length about the importance of the aura cleansing ritual. The Sphere had terrific acoustics, and I didn't miss one word, unfortunately. I'd thought her harangue about a healthy body being essential to house a healthy spirit was notably eye-glazing, but this mini-lecture was tedious to the point of pain. Even the charm of her Southern accent didn't help.

Keeping my eyes resolutely on Emmaline's face, I let my mind wander to last night with Stella. I had to concentrate to avoid a smile spoiling my expression of rapt attention. I'd found playing Ann Meadows, uptight, inexperienced heterosexual, surprisingly rewarding. It did take some effort, though, to disguise the fact I'd made love like this so many times before.

Stella had flung herself into my seduction with gratifying enthusiasm and had appeared to enjoy a feeling of warm achievement when she had finally been able to coax me into a jolting orgasm. I know she definitely enjoyed the aftermath, when Ann, brought to such unexpected heights of ecstasy, was more than willing to take instruction in order to return the favor.

I would have no qualms about telling Cynthia about the encounter, as I had no emotional ties to Stella. And, more importantly, it had been a valuable night in terms of information gained.

The reverberation of the sound of a gong broke into my thoughts. Thankfully Emmaline had at last come to the end of her address. A recording of chanting voices swelled through the Sphere, louder and louder until I was almost ready to put my hands over my ears. Then silence. The chanting, much softer, began again. It had an ethereal, not-of-this-world sound, which I suppose was the point.

The aura cleansing ceremony was at hand. One by one, we were instructed to kneel in front of Emmaline, who'd been given, somewhat alarmingly, a golden sword by one of her attendants. The other attendant held a golden bowl, into which Emmaline dipped her fingers.

The first in line advanced and sank to his knees. I squinted, imagining I could see his sullied aura swirling around him. Emmaline muttered something—I thought perhaps, "spot be gone"—as she sprinkled liquid from the bowl over his bowed head. Then she tapped him on the left and right shoulders with the flat of the sword. Disappointing to me, she didn't say, "Arise, Sir Lancelot."

I felt a strong impulse to chortle at this whole routine. Clearly, I'd not had enough sleep. My turn at cleansing was coming up fast, and I wasn't going to impress Emmaline if I laughed in the middle of the whole process.

Super serious, I knelt at her feet. She was wearing sandals and had pink nail polish on her toes. The words she intoned as she sprinkled me with whatever it was in the golden bowl turned out to be something that sounded like Latin. Then I was dubbed with the sword. I returned to my place in the line, my aura, hopefully, spotless.

The ceremony ended with a swelling chorus from the celestial choir, followed by a blast of trumpets. Emmaline declared us cleansed, then rapidly left the Sphere. We all trooped back to the locker rooms.

While I was changing back into slacks and a modest high-necked top, Lorna Gosling came into the locker room, obviously bursting with some news of great import. Being so short, she had to clamber onto a chair to be seen.

"Attention, please. All scheduled activities and ceremonies are suspended for the moment. Emmaline requests that everybody at Supremity Sanctuary immediately assemble in the auditorium."

As a murmur of speculation broke out about what this unexpected gathering might be about, Lorna jumped off the chair and made a beeline for me. "I'm so sorry, Ann," she said with deep regret. "I know you were looking forward to your clarity session this morning, but I'm afraid it's been cancelled because of this special meeting."

"Oh, darn. Has it?"

"We'll reschedule soon, don't worry."

"What's this special meeting about?" I asked.

"I can't say."

"But you know, Lorna, don't you? As Emmaline's assistant, I'm sure nothing is kept from you."

Lorna was such a pushover for a flattering comment. A pleased pink, she responded, "That's so true, but it doesn't mean I can divulge anything."

"I wouldn't expect you to," I said with a touch of restrained admiration.

"I can tell you one thing," she said. "Emmaline will be leaving much earlier than planned this afternoon. You'll have to be ready to go, if you plan to travel back with her in the limousine."

We joined the stream of people heading for the auditorium. "Emmaline said to put you in a front row seat," Lorna said. She looked at me closely to ascertain if I realized what an honor this was.

"Are you sure? After all, I'm very new to Supremity."

Obviously approving of my hesitancy, Lorna took my arm to steer me away from the general crowd and towards an exclusive entrance guarded by the gum-chewing Kenny.

"Emmaline sees beneath the bodily envelope," she announced as we made our way to the plush first-row seating. "Obviously you have potential in you, Ann. I've never seen her go to this much trouble over an outsider."

There were only a few people sitting in the front row. At the extreme end from me were Stella and Warwick Wallace. Paula Valentine was in the middle, with Rafe Thorne on one side and Mitchell Nash on the other. I twisted around to check out the audience. In the row behind me I recognized many of the people who'd been at the cocktail party last night. In the rest of the auditorium, almost every seat was filled. It struck me that they were all white faces—other ethnic groups were not represented.

The hum of conversation faded as the lights in the auditorium dimmed. On the stage, Emmaline, standing at a podium and illuminated by a spotlight, drew every eye.

I was ready for another yawn fest, but although Emmaline was an unforgivably dull speaker when giving a lecture on some aspect of Supremity's beliefs, I immediately discovered that in a situation like this she came alive. Her slightly husky Southern voice rang out with conviction, and her stocky body vibrated with energy as her hands jabbed at the air to emphasize key points.

"Some months ago and at considerable cost, Supremity purchased advertising time for tonight, Sunday, on all network television stations throughout the country. We paid a premium to invest in a single, five-minute program to be placed in each network's highest rated evening program. Our purpose? To spread the amazing, life-affirming news there's an answer to the spiritual hunger afflicting so many in our modern world. The answer? Supremity!"

Emmaline paused to permit a rumble of agreement to build to open applause. When it died down, she went on, "That segment will not run tonight. You ask why? Because yesterday a missile, fired by a single person on the ground, brought down a jumbo jet taking off at Sydney Airport."

She allowed the murmur of disapproval to last only a moment before breaking in with, "I share your outrage! Men, women and children incinerated, dying in agony!" She raised her arms. "Hear me now: Their dreadful suffering was unnecessary. If this country had strong, competent leadership, protections would have been in place. This despicable terrorist attack, and others like it, would never have been allowed to happen. Never!"

She dropped her arms, saying in an almost conversational voice, "Early this morning, at our Mediaplex facility here at Supremity Sanctuary, a new, hard-hitting five-minute segment was created. Distribution to all stations is occurring as I speak."

Behind Emmaline, a large screen slid down. "Here is an exclusive preview of what the citizens of Australia will be seeing this evening."

The spotlight blinked out. There was almost total darkness for a moment, then the screen filled with a series of disturbing images accompanied by discordant music. Each fragment illustrated a successful terrorist attack in Australia in the last weeks, culminating with the gut-wrenching pictures of yesterday's plane crash. As each image appeared, PREVENTABLE pulsated across the screen.

A close-up of Emmaline's square face and silver pageboy appeared, her intense, hypnotic eyes seeming to glow with a dark light. "My name is Emmaline Partlow. I speak for Supremity. You ask, what is Supremity? And what does Supremity have to do with the terrorist attacks that are tearing the very fabric of society apart? The answer? Everything!"

The screen switched to the prime minister at a recent media conference where he'd appeared even more hapless than usual. "I plead for everyone to keep calm." He added without conviction, "Be assured your government is doing everything humanly possible to apprehend these criminals."

Back to a militant Emmaline. "Everything possible? People

are dying while this man says the government is doing everything possible. While he twiddles his thumbs, what will be next? Poisoning of your water supply? A suicide bomber at your local school? Sniper attacks every day, every hour?"

The screen switched to a shot of the beautiful grounds of Supremity Sanctuary. Golden letters declared: SUPREMITY TOUCHES THE LIFE SPRING WITHIN EACH PERSON. CONQUER FEAR. CONQUER DOUBT. RELEASE THE UNDREAMED POWERS WITHIN YOU. BE STRONG. BE FEARLESS. LIVE THE LIFE YOU WERE MEANT TO LIVE. WALK UNAFRAID INTO YOUR GOLDEN FUTURE.

The prime minister appeared again, his face creased with gray anxiety. He was talking, but the audio of his voice was absent. In its place, the soundtrack had Emmaline asking, "What words describe the present leadership of Australia? Ineffectual. Inadequate. In the face of danger? Weak! Fatally weak!"

As a montage of scenes of Australia from the beaches to the outback ran, Emmaline said in grave tones, "We at Supremity pray that a leader will arise to take up the challenges that face this great nation. A leader who will bring Australia to a place of strength, peace and prosperity. A leader who will take up the sword against terrorism and strike down the subhuman brutes who at present are killing at will."

As a close-up of her face flashed onto the screen, Emmaline said with even more momentous gravity, "I pledge on behalf of Supremity, that when such a leader arises, he or she will have our total support. Such a person will deserve the support of every citizen, if Australia is to be saved from anarchy."

The screen went dark. The spotlight again illuminated Emmaline standing at the podium. The audience spontaneously rose in a standing ovation.

I joined in, of course, but could not match the frantic clapping of Lorna beside me. When the applause at last died down, Emmaline raised a hand in blessing, then left the stage.

"You know," I said to Lorna, "it strikes me that Rafe Thorne is just such a leader. Am I wrong?"

She clutched my arm. "You're *not* wrong, Ann. And you can be part of it. Be part of Right Way's Grand March to Power."

I knew the phrase had capital letters—Stella had told me that last night. She'd also used words like *authoritarian*, *dictatorial* and *fascist* when describing Thorne and his Right Way party.

"Heavens," I remarked, "Grand March sounds rather military."

"It's meant to," said Lorna, starry-eyed. "We'll be soldiers, fighting for the Right Way. Isn't it exciting?"

CHAPTER SEVENTEEN

In the middle of the afternoon, a young man found me with a message directly from Emmaline saying that she intended to leave for Sydney much earlier than originally planned. Although alternative transport could be arranged for me, she'd be very pleased if I accompanied her as she had several matters to discuss. I sent a message back announcing I'd be delighted to accept her offer.

Stella met me as I was leaving the lodge, overnight bag in hand. "You're leaving, Ann?"

"Emmaline's going back to the city early and has asked me to go with her."

Stella frowned. "I hope anything we discussed last night will remain confidential."

"You don't have to ask me to keep things quiet," I said. "I

have as much to lose as you." I looked down in embarrassment. "And I'd rather you didn't mention . . ."

"You loved it. Admit it."

"I had too much to drink," I said with dignity. "I hope we can both forget what happened."

"No way. A night to remember, Ann. I won't be forgetting it." With a sly smile, she added, "You up for a return bout?"

"No! I intend to put the whole thing out of my mind."

Laughing, she said, "Your body, however, might find it difficult to forget."

I dropped my voice to say, "Stella, speaking seriously, I believe I may have said rather too much last night about why I'm at *The Trump*."

She shrugged. "We both have secrets. Let's leave it at that."

Last night, to encourage Stella to speak freely, and once I was sure she had every reason not to betray me to *The Trump*, I confided several things to her, none true.

I'd told her I'd wrangled my position at the newspaper because I was, in actuality, working for Senator Conway Colby. Colby was a member of the prime minister's party and made no secret of his scorn for his leader and his desire to supplant him in the top position. That Senator Colby would recruit someone from the intelligence community like Ann Meadows was well within the realm of possibility since he had served in several government positions dealing with national security.

"Conway Colby?" Stella had said with a sneer. "He's all ambition and no ability."

I'd agreed with her, but added, "He pays well, and since my husband died . . . Well, let's just say things are difficult."

My mission, I told her, was twofold. First, I was to gather anything derogatory about the prime minister. In particular, I was to look for items that the press wouldn't publish because of

Australia's draconian libel laws. Under the protection of parliamentary privilege, Colby intended to undermine his leader with any scurrilous material I could dig up. Second, I was to provide him with up-to-the-moment information on terrorist attacks before publication so Colby would appear better-informed than the administration.

The scenario I painted so fitted in with Senator Colby's previous deceitful exploits that Stella seemed to have no trouble accepting the veracity of my story.

I said good-bye to Stella and made my way to the main building, where the limousine was waiting. Kenny, masticating gum as usual, took my bag and opened the door for me. I looked into his face, smiling. "Thank you, Kenny."

He barely acknowledged my pleasantry. I had the unsettling feeling that behind his impassive expression was a store of stone-cold malice.

Emmaline joined me in the limo a moment later. I was surprised to find she'd changed into the same elaborate golden robes as she'd been wearing in the recorded TV segment. She seemed uneasy, on edge, checking her watch, then snapping at Kenny to get a move on.

When we cleared the gates of the Esses, she leaned back with a sigh. "What did you think of the TV segment?"

"It was excellent. You put into words what I've been thinking for a long time, Emmaline. Something has to change. The country can't go on this way."

She gave me a long, considering look. "I'd be interested to hear your thoughts on Rafe Thorne."

To give the impression of a measured reply, I didn't answer immediately. Then I said, "I admit I was impressed. He has a presence that draws people to him."

"Could you see Rafe as the future leader of the country?"

I mused on this for a moment. "You know, Emmaline, I believe I could. I get the impression of strength, but also compassion."

She nodded soberly. "I'm making all of Supremity's resources available for his campaign, but under no circumstances must this total involvement become public knowledge. We don't want Rafe's opponents tarring him as the puppet of some fanatical religious movement."

Isn't it exactly what Rafe Thorne is? I thought. Aloud, I said, "Dreadful though these terrorist attacks are, they've been a help to Rafe, haven't they? I guess he owes some thanks to Righteous Scourge for financing them."

Emmaline gave me a sharp look. "You're not suggesting a link between Rafe and Righteous Scourge, are you?"

Astounded, I exclaimed, "Good God! Of course not!"

Satisfied, she leaned into the embrace of the limo's luxurious leather seating. "Warwick Wallace spoke to you at the barbecue last night."

I admitted this was so.

"Warwick's judgment is excellent. He's told me, Ann, he believes you have the qualities we need in our team."

"Team? Do you mean Supremity?"

She made an impatient gesture. "Not Supremity per se. The team is to support Rafe Thorne. We're assembling a number of experts in different fields, whose job it will be to analyze and refute statements made by those who oppose us. In the present state of the country, under constant terrorist attack, someone with an impeccable background in national security and intelligence will be an essential member of the team. You, Ann, possess both the skills and the experience in national security to respond immediately, providing Rafe with facts and figures to use as ammunition."

"I'm not sure what to say."

"I won't pressure you for an answer now. Please think it over. I can promise you such a position will be financially rewarding."

"I must confess that's tempting."

Emmaline smiled. "Perhaps you'll be further tempted to consider that in the future, when Rafe is in power, many plum jobs will be available. Those who helped him will not be forgotten."

She checked her watch, then called out, "Kenny?"

"We're on schedule," he said, sounding exasperated. "Leave it to me. Everything's under control."

After this exchange, Emmaline and I had a desultory conversation, mainly about the people at last night's cocktail party, but she soon fell silent.

The limo smoothly ate up the kilometers. As we neared Sydney, Emmaline became noticeably more tense. She checked her watch continually and even undid her seatbelt to lean through the window between the driver's compartment and our luxurious area to check the clock on the dashboard.

"I said it's under control," Kenny growled.

I expected her to snap at him for his surly tone, but she seemed too distracted to notice.

Refastening her seatbelt, she said to me, "Forgive me, Ann. I'm anxious about our TV segment tonight. It's so important that we get the message out that Australia is in the hands of incompetents who are clueless when it comes to dealing with terrorism."

"It's appearing in prime time," I said reassuringly. "You'll get a huge audience."

"I hope so." She checked her watch again.

Something was going to happen, and I was beginning to suspect what it might be. I tightened my own seatbelt. Gazing out the tinted windows, I could see we were already in the metropolitan area on surface streets. We'd had a good run, considering it was Sunday afternoon, although, being early, we'd missed the later heavy traffic as people returned to the city after spending the weekend away.

"Where are we, Kenny?" Emmaline asked. This time he didn't bother to answer.

Five minutes later, I caught a glimpse of a dark blue car as it roared past our limousine, then cut in front of us. Red lights flashed as it slowed to a crawl.

Kenny stood on the brakes, the limo slewed sideways with squealing tires, jolting to a stop angled against the back of the blue car.

If only I had my Glock with me! I looked around for a weapon. Nothing. Was Kenny armed?

We were jolted by another collision. Twisting around in my seat to look through the rear window, I saw, as I expected, a second vehicle had sandwiched the limo between it and the other car.

Through all this, Kenny had said nothing. Emmaline seemed frozen in place.

I shook her. "Emmaline, listen to me. Has Kenny got a gun?" She shook her head.

Two men leapt from the car in front, two from the car behind. I heard myself yell, "Kenny, it's a hijacking! Hit the pedal and get us out of here. Shove the blue car out of the way."

He hesitated until the shots rang out, stitching a row of holes along one side of the passenger compartment. Somewhere in the front of the limo glass shattered.

Kenny bellowed, "I've fucking been hit!" then revved the engine. There was the sound of rending metal, followed by horns blaring as we jerked across a lane into oncoming traffic.

Emmaline screamed. Kenny fought with the wheel and got us back to the correct side. We bumped over the curb and the engine stalled. "Ah, Jesus," he said, "I'm bleeding."

"Kenny's been shot?" Emmaline's eyes were wide. "Is it bad?"

I tossed my phone to her. "Dial one. It's set for emergency services."

I yelled to Kenny, "First aid kit?"

He groaned. "In the boot."

"Can you reach the release?"

I leapt out as the lid popped open. Looking back down the road I could see the men who'd tried to hijack us scrambling into their vehicles. By the time I heard the first, distant wail of sirens, they had gone.

The first media truck arrived almost simultaneously with the cops. I couldn't have my face appear in the media, so I grabbed a handful of tissues from the limo's passenger compartment and held them to my nose as if I'd whacked it on something during the hijacking, and it was bleeding.

I hardly needed to have gone to the bother—all attention was riveted on Emmaline. First to the patrol officers, then to the television crews—by this time, several had arrived—she declared with a brave, but deeply shaken demeanor, "It was an attempt to kidnap me! Or worse, to kill me! My driver and bodyguard, although seriously wounded, saved me!"

Actually, Kenny was not seriously wounded. I went over to check on him while the ambulance guys were assessing the damage before moving him from the driver's seat, where he was slumped, groaning. There was a lot of blood, but the injury wasn't life-threatening. Kenny had what would be called in a Western "a flesh wound." The bullet had skated across the top of his shoulder, leaving a deep and painful groove, but no vital damage.

In a way, Kenny was lucky to be whisked away to hospital, because for Emmaline and me the whole tiresome routine took hours. Not that she seemed to mind. She was clearly milking the whole situation for the maximum publicity, particularly when she declared the attempted hijacking was designed to silence her because of the television segment Supremity was running that very night.

After our statements were taken at the nearest police station, Emmaline and I got into another Supremity limousine, which had almost miraculously appeared. I was thoroughly exhausted, and Emmaline was talked out, so we sat in silence until I was dropped off at my flat.

Inside, I dumped my bag on the floor and called Cynthia immediately. My heart gave a little skip when I heard her voice. "Courtney, it's me," I said. "I've just got home."

"Ann, you're okay? The news gave the only casualty as the chauffeur."

"I'm fine, but how did you know I was in the limo?"

"Logically I thought you were likely to be the third person, since you traveled to the Sanctuary with Emmaline Partlow on Saturday. Plus one of the channels showed you in long shot walking away from the camera. Just a fleeting glimpse, but I'd know you anywhere."

That last comment gave me a ridiculous little thrill. Businesslike, I said, "So the story's made the TV news in a big way?"

"It sure has. That woman puts on a great performance."

"You're right to call it a performance. The whole hijacking was a set-up."

I told her about Emmaline's anxious obsession about the time and whether we were on schedule. "She was tense as hell, waiting for it to happen."

"Rather extreme to have Kenny Dowd shot," Cynthia observed dryly.

"I'm sure it was unintentional. The hijacking was all the-atrics. For one thing, there was no point in spraying the vehicle with bullets, except for dramatic effect. Nothing came close to us. And if, as she claimed, Emmaline was the target, they would have wrenched open the door and either killed her where she sat, or dragged her out to kidnap her. The whole thing was for show."

"For what purpose? What was the show for?"

"Publicity," I said. "The hijacking was carried out early enough for the TV stations to cover it in the evening news. You've seen the telecasts. Emmaline mentioned the Supremity five-minute program was running in prime time tonight, didn't she? How many people, after seeing this on the news, out of sheer curiosity will make a point of seeing it?"

"I'm curious myself," said Cynthia. "Do you know what it covers?"

I described the contents of the segment, and how I'd watched it in the auditorium with a wildly enthusiastic audience.

"It seems to me it achieves three things," Cynthia said. "It promotes Supremity and Emmaline Partlow, it ridicules the present government, and finally, without naming him, it endorses Rafe Thorne."

"And it does all this to high ratings," I added.

We went on to discuss the efforts to find the perpetrators. Cynthia had the up-to-date information. Both federal and state law enforcement were involved, and because Emmaline was an American citizen, and the incident had the hallmarks of an attempted terrorist kidnapping, the FBI had taken an interest too.

Unfortunately, it appeared the hijackers had got clean away. The vehicles they'd used had not been located, and witnesses in the area at the time had offered confused and conflicting accounts. I hadn't got a good look at any of them, so could provide no meaningful descriptions to the police. Nor could

Emmaline. When asked what she had seen, she'd wrung her hands. "I wish I could help you, but the whole shocking experience is just a blur."

"I guarantee when Kenny Dowd is interviewed, he'll have seen nothing either," I said.

Cynthia still had to debrief me on the events of the weekend, but as I'd called her the moment I'd got in the door, I hadn't even had a mug of coffee to pep me up.

I said, "I'm really tired. Can I have a break for a few minutes to get a caffeine fix? I'll call you back."

"Two things before you go. First, we've been liaising with the FBI about Roanna Aylmer."

I had a suspicion I wasn't going to like what I was about to hear. "And? What about her?"

"As you know, she's running the family business." Cynthia's voice was cool, matter-of-fact. "The Aylmer Island Resort suffered a great deal of damage in a cyclone last year and had inadequate insurance to cover the costs of rebuilding. Part of the island was closed off for months. Roanna borrowed heavily. When bookings didn't pick up as expected, the family company slid further into a financial hole."

"How much further?"

"Bankruptcy's possible."

"So Roanna really needs this deal with *The Austral Trumpeter*?"

"She really does."

Why hadn't Roanna told me? Cynthia didn't ask the question, but I was sure she was thinking it. Wanting to get off the subject as quickly as possible, I said, "You mentioned two things. What's the other one?"

She didn't immediately answer, and her silence chilled me. "It's Martin, isn't it?"

"Yes."

"What? Tell me."

"I've been monitoring his progress. His wife doesn't know, of course. He had a setback yesterday. He's back on full life support."

This was like a horrible replay of my conversation with Cynthia when she'd first told me my brother was in hospital.

"Can I go to him?"

"Denise, no. It was a risk last time. We can't run it again."

"But I can call Pam, as long as I use this safe phone?"

"Of course." She was silent for a moment, then she said, "I wish . . . If you weren't on assignment . . ."

"It's okay," I said. "I'll get back to you after I speak with Pam."

CHAPTER EIGHTEEN

The table in the conference room was strewn with copies of that morning's newspaper. Under Stella Rohm's byline, ASSASSINATION ATTEMPT: RELIGIOUS LEADER TARGETED headed the front page story of the botched hijacking. There was an excellent photograph of Emmaline beside the limousine. She was indicating the row of bullet holes, her face and stance expressing a rather effective combination of distress and brave resolve.

"Pity Emmaline hogged the camera," Alec Slater said to me, "with you being so photogenic and all."

I ignored his leer and replied sincerely, "Thank you, Alec, for the compliment. It's very nice of you to say so."

On the other side of the conference table, Brad Thomson chuckled. "I reckon Ann's got your measure, mate."

Stella strode in, slamming the door behind her. "The leaders of the Coolangatta Five have just been arrested, minutes before they triggered an explosion in a petrol tanker in a repeat of their most successful exploit in the seventies. I've got Jon and Francesca out in the field."

"Hell, the Coolangatta Five must be middle-aged by now," Brad remarked. "Rather old to be traipsing around blowing up tankers."

I couldn't resist chiming in with, "Couldn't that be an angle for a story: baby boomer bombers?"

"Not bad," Stella conceded. "I'll bear it in mind."

She flicked us copies of the item on the wire service. "You'll notice it happened in Rafe Thorne's district. He's claiming his Terrorist Watch organization was instrumental in the arrests. Jon and Francesca are covering that aspect."

She jabbed a finger at me. "Ann, use your contacts. I want the facts on how the Feds, ASIO, whatever, were involved in getting these bastards. Alec, work with her—I want an upbeat take on how the intelligence agencies, in spite of government paralysis, are working hard to contain this wave of urban terrorism."

She turned to Brad. "You're flying to Canberra this morning. The PM's spin merchants have him scheduled to do a photo op and stirring speech in front of Parliament House about the capture of the Coolangatta Five. It'll be his usual 'the tide is turning, blah, blah, blah' speech. He's taking questions afterwards. You know what to do."

Alec ran a hand over his balding dome. With a suggestive smile, he said to me, "Working very closely with you will be such a pleasure."

"I can guarantee the pleasure's all yours," I snapped.

"Oh, yes, she's definitely got your measure," Brad chortled.

Stella had no time for banter. "Let's get to work, people. Brad, a car's waiting to take you to the airport."

157

She strode out of the room with the same nervy energy with which she'd entered. Brad hastened after her.

Alec snickered. "Stella's like a greyhound, champing at the bit," he declared.

"Mixed metaphor," I said. "Beats me how you passed journalism one-o-one."

Alec's grin faded. He shot me a venomous look. I gave myself a mental slap. I had to work with this guy, so why was I sparring with him?

I was about to say something conciliatory, when Alec said jeeringly, "That time of the month, is it? Can't cope?"

Conciliation turned up its toes and died.

Back at my desk, I read through the wire report. It was succinct, containing the bare details of the arrest which had occurred in Parramatta this morning. Three men and a woman had been in a car following a fully-loaded tanker as it made its first scheduled delivery to a large service station in a high-density residential area. A bomb had been concealed underneath the tanker. When apprehended, the suspects had in their possession a radio device to detonate it from a safe distance.

Putting my hand on my phone to ring my multi-person ASIO intelligence contact, Tony Scott, I paused, wishing I could risk a call to Pam on this unsecured line.

I'd reached Pam on her cell phone last night, finding her, as I expected, at the hospital. There'd been no change in Martin's condition from Saturday, but at least he wasn't any worse.

"Pam, I'm so sorry, but at the moment I can't come to see him," I'd said.

Her voice had been tired, defeated. "I understand, Denise."

I knew she didn't. Perhaps one day I could explain how visiting my critically ill brother had the potential to fatally compromise my undercover assignment. Perhaps not.

This morning, before leaving for *The Trump*, I'd called Pam again.

"Martin's had a good night," she said. "The doctor's cautiously optimistic. I'll know more in a couple of hours when the lab reports are in."

I could tell from Pam's voice she was hardly daring to hope he would recover. "He's turned the corner. I'm sure," I assured her. Empty words, but they seemed to offer some comfort.

Before I rang off, Pam said, "Denise, when Martin's better, you'll come and see him, won't you?"

Only if he wants to see me, I thought. Then I was ashamed. That was the way both Martin and I had behaved—always waiting for the other to make concessions.

"Absolutely I will," I said. "As soon as he's well enough, I'll be there."

"Stella?"

She looked up from her desk. Her blond hair was sleeked back, her athletic body poised on the chair as if she were ready for forceful action.

"Got something?"

I nodded. "I have."

She leaned back to regard me. "For me? Or for *The Trump*?"

"Maybe both."

She indicated a chair. "Sit."

As I'd told Cynthia last night, at the Esses Stella had confided to me rather more than she'd intended. I was deliberately vague over how this had come about, implying it was champagne-induced, but I didn't fool Cynthia. She made a wry comment about sex and secrets, but there was nothing of the harsh reaction she'd had to my liaison with Roanna.

"Stella Rohm is writing a book!" Cynthia had exclaimed. I could imagine her expression at the other end of the phone. Her expressive eyebrows would be raised, her mouth would be quirked in a half-smile.

"Not a novel. A serious nonfiction she's writing under a pseudonym. Her literary agent has negotiated a contract with a large publisher. The working title is *Corruption Within: The Rise and Fall of Democracy in Australia.*"

I'd gone on to explain how Stella's career in journalism had exposed her to the dark underside of politics and power. She had become imbued with a burning desire to break through the average citizen's apathy and ignorance by exposing the corruption and expediency she'd discovered at the highest levels of government and industry.

When Stella had been recruited by a headhunter for the position of deputy managing editor at *The Austral Trumpeter*, she'd already been aware of a covert association among Rafe Thorne, Jason Benton and Emmaline Partlow. She'd accepted the job offer with alacrity and had been secretly gathering material ever since.

Looking at her this Monday morning—crisp, abrupt, wound tight with purpose—it was hard to reconcile her with the woman with whom I'd shared my bed on Saturday night.

"What have you got?" she asked once I was seated.

"There was no national security involvement until this morning. No one in any intelligence organization had any idea that the Coolangatta Five were about to explode that tanker. Files were still open on the group, but the only recent material related to rumors they'd got together again and perhaps were planning terrorist activity."

"So it was Thorne's Terrorist Watch who blew the whistle?"

Stella snorted in disgust. "He's going to milk this for all it's worth—and it's worth a lot."

"The guy who heads the Terrorist Watch, Phil O'Reilly, was the one who passed on to the Federal Police and the local cops the where and when and how of the attack, but it's not altogether clear how he got the information," I said. "O'Reilly himself has got quite a shady background. Never indicted, but arrested in Northern Ireland several times for suspected involvement in partisan attacks. That's a trail that might be worth following."

"Maybe a member of the Five got cold feet and leaked information on the strike," Stella said.

"Or perhaps Righteous Scourge did the betraying," I said. "If the Coolangatta Five wanted to be considered for that tempting cash reward the Web site offers, they would first have to come up with a detailed, viable plan, so Righteous Scourge, or someone associated with them, would have all the details."

She rubbed her forehead thoughtfully. "We don't know if they did apply to Righteous Scourge in the first place."

Oliver Yorkin bounced through the door. Like many little men sensitive about lack of height, he stood as tall as possible. "Attention, Stella!" he boomed in his too-large voice. "Our revered publisher wants you and anyone on your team who's available in the conference room, quick smart."

"I haven't time for this. What does Jason want?"

"Editorial policy." His cheerful expression changed to a scowl. "Christ! Being the managing editor of opinion sucks at times. I've got a fair idea what Jason's on about, enough to know I'm not going to be happy."

Stella sighed as she got to her feet. "It's Rafe Thorne, isn't it?"

"I'm guessing so. Bloody fascist—" He did an elaborate mime of zippering his lips. Then he laughed. "I never said that."

161

"Ann, collect Alec, will you?"

Alec was in his cubicle, leaning back in his chair, his feet on his desk, talking on the phone. " . . . and then I said to this piece of shit, so she's your wife. What of it? She's still got bloody good tits. And he said—" He broke off when he saw me. "Mate, I'll call you later. Someone else with bloody good tits has just come in."

"The compliments never end," I said, contemplating a quick blow to the Adam's apple or maybe a snap kick to the kneecap.

"What can I do for you?" he asked with his trademark leer.

"Mr. Benton has called a meeting in the conference room."

Alec swung his feet off the desk and onto the floor. "It'll be about that bastard, Thorne." He gestured at his computer monitor. "The Coolangatta Five arrests have lifted him to another level. He's on the Internet, he's everywhere—radio, television, you name it. The savior of the common man. The one who can do what the PM can't—foil a terrorist attack."

When we got to the meeting, I found we were the last to come in. I looked around the room. There were several people there I knew only by sight. Jason Benton was seated at the head of the conference table. I was surprised to see Roanna beside him, looking bored. Paula Valentine was there, as, oddly I thought, was her husband, Mitchell Nash. Stella and Oliver were seated together, chatting. Also present were Warwick Wallace, Emmaline and Lorna.

Jason Benton cleared his throat. That was enough to silence conversation. Everyone looked at him expectantly.

"I've called you here today, to announce a change in editorial policy." His ugly face was blank, and he spoke in his usual, very soft monotone. "In its short life, *The Austral Trumpeter* has never taken political sides editorially, but that will change beginning now. As publisher and CEO, and after consultation with Emmaline Partlow, I have decided that recent events indicate we should unambiguously support Rafe Thorne and his Right Way party."

He indicated Mitchell Nash, who turned his head to flash a smile at as many people as possible. "Mitchell will act as our liaison with Right Way."

"This is just in editorial pages?" Oliver Yorkin asked. "Is that right?"

Benton took his time answering. "The entire newspaper must reflect my editorial policy. If an item is critical of Thorne or Right Way, it doesn't matter if it's categorized as news or opinion, it must cross my desk before being considered for publication."

This statement caused a murmur in the room. Jason Benton put up his hand to quiet the comments. "I'm aware that this policy may run counter to political views some of you hold. I will be happy to arrange a generous severance package for any who find themselves unable, in good conscience, to work for this newspaper."

Indicating Paula Valentine, he added, "Please direct any questions to Paula. She will be delighted to answer any concerns that you have."

During the rather heated session that followed, I saw Roanna get up and leave the room. Thinking this would be a good opportunity to speak with her, I slipped out too. Ann Meadows was not supposed to know Roanna, but of course we would have run into each other in the newsroom, so a quick conversation would look quite natural.

When I caught up with her, I said, "Can I see you for a moment?"

She looked at me guardedly. "What is it?"

"Why didn't you tell me the resort was in financial trouble?"

Roanna blushed. I'd never seen her embarrassed before. "I didn't think you'd be interested."

"Of course I'm interested. What's the situation?"

She shrugged. "I need working capital. Jason's considering investing, but we're still stuck at the negotiation stage."

A knot of people came out of the meeting, all talking at once. I allowed myself to be swept up with them. Looking back, I saw Roanna staring after me, an expression on her face I couldn't read.

Back in my cubicle, it came to me what it was. Guilt.

CHAPTER NINETEEN

Two days later, I was in Brad's cubicle helping him with an article he was writing on international cooperation between the various national intelligence services, when sounds of a violent argument caught our attention. We weren't the only ones. People were popping out of offices and looking down the corridor towards Emmaline's office.

"You fat bitch!" shouted a female voice. "You and your bloody cult made Rafe fire me!"

"Nancy Otega," said Brad to me, grimacing. "They call her Hatchet Mary. Looks like she's getting some of her own medicine."

Emmaline's unmistakable tones followed. "You stupid, stupid woman! I didn't make Rafe do anything."

"Don't lie to me! You've brainwashed him. He'll do anything you tell him to."

"Rafe's better off without you." Emmaline's voice dripped with scorn. "The heights he'll reach in the future are well beyond your paltry level of PR competence."

Choked with rage, Nancy Otega ground out, "You won't get away with this! I'll make you pay."

"Is that a threat?"

"It's a promise, you bitch, it's a promise. There are things I know—"

"Get off the premises or I'll have you arrested."

A door slammed and the diminutive Nancy Otega, her face white with rage, stormed down the corridor. Before disappearing into the reception area, she turned and yelled, "I'll get you for this!"

Alec came sauntering along, grinning. "Best entertainment I've had all day."

Brad's phone rang. "For you," he said, handing me the receiver.

"It's June Smythe here," said a voice I didn't know. "It's ages since we've met, Ann. Are you free for lunch next week?"

"I'll have to get back to you," I said. "It's a madhouse around here at the moment."

I finished with Brad, took the list of questions he wanted answered and went back to my desk to get my keys. June's message meant I had to speak with Cynthia on a secure line at the earliest possible moment.

I told Jon I had to run an errand and if anyone wanted me, I'd be back shortly, and went down to my car. Out of force of habit I didn't hurry—people tended to remember someone in obvious haste.

My flat looked even more commonplace and dull by day than by night. I got myself a glass of water, sat down on the standard-issue lounge chair and dialed Cynthia's number.

"What is it?" I said when she answered.

"After all this time, Harry Aylmer's finally talking."

"Is he? Why?"

Roanna's brother, like her parents, had held out, refusing to give any useful information, even when offered considerable improvements in the conditions of their captivity.

"He's been offered a reduction in his sentence plus extra privileges and a move to the same federal prison his mother is in, with a guarantee they'll meet at least occasionally."

Harry Aylmer was a traitor, and fortunate there was no death penalty in Australia. "That's very generous. I hope his information was worth it."

"He's spelled it all out. Tied Benton and Emmaline Partlow together. The whole elaborate scheme was hatched years ago and discussed at length in meetings at the Aylmer Resort."

I dreaded to hear the answer to my next question, but I had to ask it. "Was Roanna involved in these discussions?"

"He refused to discuss his sister." Cynthia sounded weary.

"Are you okay?" I asked.

"I'm fine. I'll run through the key points for you."

Cynthia did her usual excellent job of summarizing clearly and concisely. The conspiracy was breathtaking in its audacity and extent, and it all started with Emmaline Partlow and the astonishing success of Supremity, which gave her huge sums of money to play with.

Emmaline's ambitions were global. She had a ravenous appetite for power and saw politics at its highest reaches as a means to obtain it. Her own country, America, presented many obstacles to wholesale political manipulation, so she decided to experiment on a smaller, more manageable country. She considered Canada, but ultimately decided that Australia, having a political system friendly to small parties, would be ideal to test her strategies.

Righteous Scourge was Emmaline's brainchild and integral

to her scheme to install a puppet leader who would do her bidding. The Web site was created and run by two computer experts who were high up in Supremity's ranks. Harry Aylmer said that initially Emmaline had believed that it would be necessary to hire criminals to carry out some of the terrorist attacks, but he was of the opinion that Righteous Scourge had found enough homegrown terrorists to make this unnecessary.

And Jason Benton? As hungry for global influence as Emmaline and with the identical contempt for democratic ideals, Benton saw his personal path to power was through control of the media. Philosophically he was on the same page, but what clinched his support was Emmaline's undertaking not only to help bankroll *The Austral Trumpeter*, but to financially assist the creation of an international media empire.

Once Supremity was established in Australia, Emmaline looked for a suitable right-wing politician, heading a small party with growing political clout. She required a smooth and prepossessing individual, preferably completely amoral, who would gladly trade his or her soul for the chance to get to the top. A person who would accept, at least at first, that Emmaline was the power behind the throne. Once the structure had been created, the prime minister, should he or she become troublesome, would be deposed, and someone more acquiescent would be installed.

Of course, being personable and ambitious was not enough to guarantee the top job. This was where the media could be used to advantage. Once the country had been thoroughly terrified by the avalanche of random murders and the elected government was reeling, Emmaline's handpicked politician would foil a potentially horrific terrorist attack, then ride the wave of media attention and public approval to victory in the election that would follow a parliamentary vote of no confidence.

From Emmaline's point of view, Rafe Thorne was the perfect candidate.

"All this is hearsay," Cynthia said. "Harry Aylmer's testimony is not enough. We have no hard evidence. We can arrest some people on the periphery of Supremity, but we need to nail the principals, Partlow and Benton."

"I'm working on it," I said. "There's a meeting at Emmaline's penthouse tomorrow night to set up Rafe Thorne's war room. I've been offered the position of national security advisor."

"The penthouse is a hardened target. It's totally protected. It's impossible to get anyone in to bug the place, and tapping the phones has got us absolutely nowhere."

"Then you need my eyes and ears all the more," I declared.

I heard her sigh. "Be careful. You could be compromised at any moment, either by design or accident."

With a pulse of anger, I snapped, "Don't beat around the bush. Come out and say you mean Roanna."

"Just be careful."

Before Cynthia rang off, I told her about the argument between Emmaline and Nancy Otega and the threats Nancy had made.

"I'll follow it up," she said. "Maybe Ms. Otega will be happy to talk to us."

CHAPTER TWENTY

When I arrived at the penthouse for the meeting of Rafe Thorne's prospective war room candidates, I was greeted by Lorna Gosling. Tonight there was no Roman look. Instead of tunic and sandals, she wore a demure, dark blue dress. "Emmaline has asked me to take the minutes of the meeting," she said. "It's such an honor!"

Then, disconcertingly, she took my hand and looked deeply into my eyes. "Tomorrow is a new, promising day," she said.

"Pardon?"

"Life is a precious gift."

"Lorna, why are you telling me this?"

"You mustn't let things get you down. Remember, there's always Supremity."

"A great comfort to know that," I said dryly.

Naturally Lorna took my comment at face value. "It *is* a comfort. I'm so glad you see that."

The meeting was to be held in a comfortable sitting room, furnished in the palest of lavender shades. I established myself on a plush sofa and checked out who was present. There were already several people there, most of whom I didn't know, although I recognized a few faces from the weekend at the Esses. As Lorna introduced me, I repeated each name politely, to fix it in my memory.

Rafe Thorne came in, smiling, with Warwick Wallace by his side. I had to admit the politician had a magnetic appeal, as his very presence energized the room. Rafe was accustomed to being the golden center of attention, and he basked in the warm approval that greeted him.

When Emmaline entered, a different reaction occurred. Rafe Thorne was charismatic. Emmaline was feared and admired. She did the circuit of the room, and when she got to me, said, "Ann, feeling better?"

"I feel fine, thank you."

Warwick Wallace called everyone to order, Lorna opened her laptop and sat, fingers poised, ready to take down every detail for the minutes. Emmaline, of course, chaired the meeting. She was excellent in the position, controlling the flow of information, adroitly cutting off the blatherers, emphasizing important issues, giving credit where credit was due, but never hesitating to be critical when it was appropriate.

I was impressed by the caliber of the people present. The broad general areas of economics, healthcare, education, law enforcement, national security, the armed forces and social issues were covered by individuals who clearly knew their areas.

"This is a preliminary meeting, one of many," said Emmaline, winding up the proceedings. "Please stay here and chat among yourselves. Refreshments will be served in a few moments." She nodded to Lorna, who took the cue and hurried off in the direction of the kitchen.

A middle-aged man—I recalled his name was Edward Burton—came over to sit by me on the sofa.

"Things will get better, Ann. The dark before the dawn and all that."

"I beg your pardon?" I said.

"I felt the same way when my wife died. Some days I thought I couldn't go on. But time heals, it really does."

I was puzzled at this sudden solicitude, but said what seemed to be expected of me. "Bill's death was an awful shock, even though he'd been ill for so long. Although he's gone, I have my memories . . ."

"Of course you do. Wonderful memories." He patted my hand with a kind, understanding expression on his face. "You mustn't allow yourself to get too depressed, Ann. Don't be ashamed to ask for help. A short-term course of medication can be a lifesaver. Literally."

I looked at him, flabbergasted. "Are you thinking I'm suicidal? Whatever gave you that idea?"

Edward reddened. "If I've spoken out of turn, forgive me, please. It's just that Emmaline has been so worried about you. She felt if you embraced Supremity fully this deep depression would lift, but that hasn't happened. It's clear something dark in your inner core is attempting to destroy you."

I shivered involuntarily. Lorna's words took on a new significance. Was Emmaline intending to do away with me? Perhaps drug me, so I'd be found dead in my flat? No farewell note was necessary, because it wasn't true that those who killed themselves always left some written explanation. Although, knowing Emmaline, she'd be quite capable of going to the trouble of providing a forged suicide note plus plenty of witnesses who'd speak movingly of my inability to cope with the death of my nearest and dearest. Too bad Bill didn't exist—but Emmaline didn't know that. Or did she? I had a sudden flash of Roanna's face the last time I'd seen her.

"I don't have something dark in my inner core," I declared. "And I'm not planning to kill myself."

"Of course you're not." It was patently obvious he was humoring me. He took out his wallet and handed over his business card. "Call anytime. I'd be happy to provide a sympathetic ear. Talking things out can be such a comfort, Ann. I know it helped me after Norma passed away."

"Excuse me for interrupting you."

I looked up into Emmaline's face. She was smiling warmly.

"Ann and I were just having a little chat," Edward said meaningfully, making it obvious Emmaline had set up the conversation.

Emmaline smiled a little more. "That's nice. Ann? If I could have a quick word in private?"

Wary, I left the sitting room and followed her down the hallway into the most spectacular room in the penthouse, where the views of the city and harbor were almost overwhelming in their magnificence.

"What is it?" I asked.

"A serious matter, I'm afraid."

I heard a slight noise and turned to see Kenny approaching with slow, deliberate steps, his jaws moving rhythmically as he chewed his ubiquitous gum. He had no weapon I could see, but he held his hands away from his body, his stance telegraphing that he was ready to move against me.

I kept my eyes on Kenny, while I spoke to Emmaline. "What serious matter?"

"I don't take betrayal lightly, Ann. I'm very disappointed."

"What's Kenny here for? To throw me out?"

Kenny snorted a laugh. "Not *out*," he said.

He was much stronger and heavier than I, but I thought I could deal with him if I had the element of surprise. It would be better to avoid the confrontation altogether, if I could. Escape routes? The balcony was out of the question as I'd be trapped there. And Kenny was blocking the way to the doorway to the hall.

"How am I supposed to have betrayed you, Emmaline?"

As I spoke, I assessed the situation. There was a heavy purple vase holding mauve roses on a table at the end of the couch. In a pinch, it could be a weapon. And the furniture could help me. Surely I'd be quicker on my feet than Kenny and could dodge him, using the couch and chairs as barriers.

My mistake was to think Kenny would be the one to physically attack me. Out of the corner of my eye I saw Emmaline raise her arm, and turned too late. With preternatural clarity, I watched the wicked little blackjack whip through the air.

I was moving my head back, but not fast enough. The blow fell with dreadful force. I must have heard the dull crack as it hit my skull, but remember only the pain lancing through me and the darkness rushing to fill my eyes. I felt my muscles loosen, then my knees gave way, and I fell, face down, onto the purple carpet.

I couldn't move, and although I tried to open my eyes, I couldn't see. But hearing, I remembered distantly, was the last sense to go when losing consciousness and the first to return.

"Kenny! Don't let her bleed on the carpet."

A rustle of something, then my head was lifted for a moment. "That takes care of it."

"Make sure any spots are cleaned up immediately."

Kenny grunted affirmatively.

"And give me time to get back to the group, so I'm nowhere near her when she falls. Five minutes, then throw her over.

Head first would be best, so any damage I've done to her skull is obliterated in the fall."

"Right."

"Five minutes, Kenny. After you've got rid of her, go down the hall to the TV room and wait there. I'll say to everyone, 'Isn't that a scream?' and then I'll come out and call you to investigate, so you must be in position."

"Ah, Jesus, Emmaline, I've got it straight! Get going before the bitch wakes up."

I had five minutes. Some sensation was returning to my body. My head was pounding, but I ignored that. What was important was that I could feel against my cheek the slick texture of whatever it was Kenny had put under my head to keep blood off the carpet. I opened my eyes a slit. It was plastic. Cautiously, I moved my fingers slightly. Concealed by my shoes, I wiggled my toes.

At this point I could hardly provide anything more than token resistance. I'd feign complete unconsciousness until the last moment, waiting for my strength to return. *Please God make it return in time*.

I heard Kenny open the glass doors to the balcony. He came back to me and with a grunt, lifted me into a sitting position. I lolled, eyes closed, mouth half open.

Walking backwards, he dragged me out through the doors and onto the cold tiles of the balcony, where he dumped me so unceremoniously that my head bounced on the floor. Pain exploded behind my eyes, but I remained inert, faking unconsciousness.

Warm blood was running down the side of my face. I could hear the soft plunk as it dripped onto the tiles. Ridiculously, I spent a moment musing on what an inefficient killer Kenny made. Apart from the drops on the carpet from when he dragged me out here, there'd be a pool of blood on the balcony tiles, something difficult to account for in the scenario Emmaline obviously intended to give the police investigating my apparent suicide.

I heard the scrape of a match and realised Kenny was enjoying a few drags of a cigarette before dispatching me. Up to now, I hadn't realized that he smoked. Perhaps that's why he always chewed gum.

I had the stray thought that it was the condemned person who was allowed a last cigarette, not the executioner.

I opened my eyes a crack. Kenny was leaning with his elbows on the railing, smoking. He checked his watch and gave an impatient grunt. Then he went to throw his half-smoked cigarette away, but changed his mind. Putting it in the corner of his mouth to leave both hands free, he came over to me.

Even for someone as strong as Kenny, a limp body with flopping limbs was hard to handle. He maneuvered me until I was sitting with my back to the railing. He straddled my legs and putting his hands under my armpits, began to heave me up, to sit my slack body on the top of the railing. Then it would be easy to give me a shove, so I toppled over backwards.

It was a horrible parody of a romantic clinch. We were face to face, so close I could feel the heat from his cigarette.

I opened my eyes wide. We stared at each other. Then I seized the cigarette and plunged the glowing tip into his right eye.

He bellowed in agony, and staggered back. I fell to my knees, dragged myself up by hanging on to the railing, and stumbled towards the glass doors.

With one hand covering his eye, Kenny came after me. I'd made it to the couch when he caught me. I twisted in his grip and with a desperate heave, reached for the heavy ceramic vase.

Raising it in both hands, I smashed the vase over his head with all that remained of my strength. He fell to his hands and knees, groaning. In a moment, he'd recover and would kill me with his bare hands.

I screamed as Ann would scream, high and shrill. And then I shrieked, "Rape! Rape! Help me! Someone help me!"

It had the desired effect. Everyone piled into the room to gape at the astonishing sight of me, blood pouring down my face, standing over Kenny Dowd who, on hands and knees, was surrounded by shards of purple ceramic and scattered mauve roses.

CHAPTER TWENTY-ONE

Roanna refused to see me after her arrest for conspiracy to commit murder. It was an initial charge to hold her while Australia's security services and the FBI gathered evidence for more serious indictments, including espionage and, in the case of the FBI, Roanna's possible involvement in the deaths of two American agents.

Keith Francis, my boss, had been present during her interrogations. When he saw me later, he told me he had videos of the sessions, or, if I preferred not to view them, he'd simply tell me what Roanna had said about her betrayal of me to Jason Benton.

I chose to watch the videos. Keith had indicated the section where Roanna discussed why she'd outed me as an undercover agent. I had security clearance to take the videos out of the building, but I didn't want to see it at home—I wasn't sure why—so I found an empty viewing room and sat down alone with a remote control in my hand. A long time passed before I started the video.

Interrogation tapes were not designed to flatter, but Roanna looked as attractive as ever, with her dark hair and subtly rebellious manner. Some questions she declined to answer, but when she was asked about Agent Denise Cleever, she spoke freely, looking directly into the camera.

"I had no idea that Denise was about to go undercover at *The Trump* before I came to ASIO with information about Jason Benton and Righteous Scourge. Why did I do it? Because I was sickened by the terrorist violence." She smiled slightly. "Perhaps you find that hard to believe, given the things you've accused me of, but it's the truth."

Someone off camera asked an inaudible question. Roanna shook her head. "No, I didn't think by doing that I was betraying Jason. It was my parents and my two brothers who were involved with Jason and Emmaline Partlow, not me."

She went on to describe the business relationship she had with Jason Benton and *The Austral Trumpeter*. "Aylmer Resort was bleeding money. I've lived there all my life, and I was desperate to save it, not just for me, but for my family, too. The joint venture with *The Trump* wasn't going to be enough. I asked Jason for a substantial loan. I even offered a share of the business."

She shrugged. "Essentially Jason stonewalled, while the resort was sliding fast to financial ruin." With a bitter smile, she added, "I guess he thought if he waited, he'd pick up the whole island at a bargain-basement price."

I recognized Keith's voice saying, "You told Benton that Ann Meadows was actually an ASIO undercover agent."

Roanna looked down at her hands. "I'll regret that for the rest of my life."

"And your reward for this information?"

179

"A guaranteed loan. I had him sign the contract before I gave him Denise's undercover name." She looked up at the camera again and spoke to me. "I swear, Denise, I had no idea Emmaline would try to hurt you. Jason promised me—"

I hit the off button. Staring at the blank screen, I knew I'd never willingly see Roanna ever again.

Jason Benton and Emmaline had been arrested, charged with terrorism against the state, murder, attempted murder and a string of lesser crimes. Supremity's financial records had been seized for investigation of money laundering, tax evasion and fraud.

Kenny Dowd's initial booking was for my attempted murder and the planting of an explosive device in Nancy Otega's car to maim or kill her. Fortunately for Nancy, she had a suspicious nature, and when she had found her locked vehicle was now unaccountably unlocked, she'd called the police to say death threats had been made against her, and she believed her car had been tampered with.

Warwick Wallace was a fugitive, having fled the country. Lorna Gosling initially refused to believe that Supremity was a breathtaking scam, but once convinced, she began talking freely. With her help it was possible to identify and arrest the hijackers and the two men running the Righteous Scourge Web site. Using information gained from Righteous Scourge files, the snipers and the terrorists responsible for bringing down the passenger plane had been apprehended.

Rafe Thorne's whole organization was under investigation and his political career in tatters. So far his lawyers were successfully arguing he was too dumb to really know what was going on, but this ploy seemed destined to fail, as Mitchell Nash and his wife Paula Valentine were trading information on Thorne and Right Way on the understanding they would face lesser charges.

The Trump was up for sale.

And Stella Rohm? She'd put her book on hold and together with Jon Hong was writing a sensational expose, predicted to be a bestseller internationally, titled *Supremity Betrayed: Emmaline Partlow and the Pursuit of Power.*

I entered the hospital room with trepidation, not sure what to expect. "Martin, hi."

The basket of fruit I was holding gave me something to do with my hands. "I brought you some fruit," I said unnecessarily.

"Thank you." My brother looked emaciated and tired, but he managed a smile. "Pam says you visited me when I was in intensive care."

"Yes, I came as soon as I heard." I busied myself finding a place for the basket on the bedside table. To fill the silence, I said lightly, "Good thing you were in a Volvo."

Martin gave a soft laugh. "You've always hated those cars, Denise."

"True. But now I have quite a different view."

I stood awkwardly beside the bed, not sure what to do. Martin said, "Are you going to stay for a while?"

"Of course." I pulled up the white visitor's chair and sat down.

"I'm grateful for the support you gave to Pam," he said. "It meant a lot to her."

I felt guilty for the little I had done for Martin's wife. "I just spoke to Pam a few times on the phone. I wished I could have done more."

"She told me you were on assignment."

Martin had never approved of my career with ASIO. I said defensively, "I'm sorry, but it wasn't possible to get away."

"You're doing important work. I'm proud of you, Denise."

It was the last thing I expected my brother to say. As I stared at him, he went on, "I should have told you that long ago."

Impulsively, I leaned forward and put my hand on his. "There are a lot of things we should have said to each other, Martin."

"There are."

"Let's make up for lost time," I said, "and begin now."

Cynthia retired from ASIO with all the in-house pomp and circumstance appropriate for someone so excellent at her job.

In her Willow Trent persona, on the evening of the day she left ASIO, she had an exhibition of artwork on the theme of freedom opening at a prestigious gallery.

Willow Trent. Why was it difficult to think of Cynthia by that name? I smiled to myself, thinking I'd cope. After all, I'd known her by so many other names in the past.

I arrived at the exhibition early and introduced myself to the black-clad, very slender gallery owner, who murmured suitably upbeat remarks about the exhibition, then left me to greet the next arrivals. I took a glass of wine and wandered around. Some sculptures I liked, most I found very strange.

I heard a laugh I knew so well and turned to see that Cynthia had entered with a group of people. I watched her, fascinated. She was so individual, so alive.

Cynthia caught sight of me, and a smile illuminated her face.

In my heart, an answering light began to shine.

I'd asked myself before, could one love the artist, but not the art? The answer, it seemed, was *yes*.

WHEN LOVE FINDS A HOME by Megan Carter. 280 pp. What will it take for Anna and Rona to find their way back to each other again? 1-59493-041-4 $12.95

MEMORIES TO DIE FOR by Adrian Gold. 240 pp. Rachel attempts to avoid her attraction to the charms of Anna Sigurdson . . . 1-59493-038-4 $12.95

SILENT HEART by Claire McNab. 280 pp. Exotic lesbian romance. 1-59493-044-9 $12.95

MIDNIGHT RAIN by Peggy J. Herring. 240 pp. Bridget McBee is determined to find the woman who saved her life. 1-59493-021-X $12.95

THE MISSING PAGE A Brenda Strange Mystery by Patty G. Henderson. 240 pp. Brenda investigates her client's murder . . . 1-59493-004-X $12.95

WHISPERS ON THE WIND by Frankie J. Jones. 240 pp. Dixon thinks she and her best friend, Elizabeth Colter, would make the perfect couple . . . 1-59493-037-6 $12.95

CALL OF THE DARK: EROTIC LESBIAN TALES OF THE SUPERNATURAL edited by Therese Szymanski—from Bella After Dark. 320 pp. 1-59493-040-6 $14.95

A TIME TO CAST AWAY A Helen Black Mystery by Pat Welch. 240 pp. Helen stops by Alice's apartment—only to find the woman dead . . . 1-59493-036-8 $12.95

DESERT OF THE HEART by Jane Rule. 224 pp. The book that launched the most popular lesbian movie of all time is back. 1-1-59493-035-X $12.95

THE NEXT WORLD by Ursula Steck. 240 pp. Anna's friend Mido is threatened and eventually disappears . . . 1-59493-024-4 $12.95

CALL SHOTGUN by Jaime Clevenger. 240 pp. Kelly gets pulled back into the world of private investigation . . . 1-59493-016-3 $12.95

52 PICKUP by Bonnie J. Morris and E.B. Casey. 240 pp. 52 hot, romantic tales—one for every Saturday night of the year. 1-59493-026-0 $12.95

GOLD FEVER by Lyn Denison. 240 pp. Kate's first love, Ashley, returns to their home town, where Kate now lives . . . 1-1-59493-039-2 $12.95

RISKY INVESTMENT by Beth Moore. 240 pp. Lynn's best friend and roommate needs her to pretend Chris is his fiancé. But nothing is ever easy. 1-59493-019-8 $12.95

HUNTER'S WAY by Gerri Hill. 240 pp. Homicide detective Tori Hunter is forced to team up with the hot-tempered Samantha Kennedy. 1-59493-018-X $12.95

CAR POOL by Karin Kallmaker. 240 pp. Soft shoulders, merging traffic and slippery when wet . . . Anthea and Shay find love in the car pool. 1-59493-013-9 $12.95

NO SISTER OF MINE by Jeanne G'Fellers. 240 pp. Telepathic women fight to coexist with a patriarchal society that wishes their eradication. ISBN 1-59493-017-1 $12.95

ON THE WINGS OF LOVE by Megan Carter. 240 pp. Stacie's reporting career is on the rocks. She has to interview bestselling author Cheryl, or else! ISBN 1-59493-027-9 $12.95

WICKED GOOD TIME by Diana Tremain Braund. 224 pp. Does Christina need Miki as a protector . . . or want her as a lover? ISBN 1-59493-031-7 $12.95

THOSE WHO WAIT by Peggy J. Herring. 240 pp. Two brilliant sisters—in love with the same woman! ISBN 1-59493-032-5 $12.95

ABBY'S PASSION by Jackie Calhoun. 240 pp. Abby's bipolar sister helps turn her world upside down, so she must decide what's most important. ISBN 1-59493-014-7 $12.95

PICTURE PERFECT by Jane Vollbrecht. 240 pp. Kate is reintroduced to Casey, the daughter of an old friend. Can they withstand Kate's career? ISBN 1-59493-015-5 $12.95

PAPERBACK ROMANCE by Karin Kallmaker. 240 pp. Carolyn falls for tall, dark and . . . female . . . in this classic lesbian romance. ISBN 1-59493-033-3 $12.95

DAWN OF CHANGE by Gerri Hill. 240 pp. Susan ran away to find peace in remote Kings Canyon—then she met Shawn . . . ISBN 1-59493-011-2 $12.95

DOWN THE RABBIT HOLE by Lynne Jamneck. 240 pp. Is a killer holding a grudge against FBI Agent Samantha Skellar? ISBN 1-59493-012-0 $12.95

SEASONS OF THE HEART by Jackie Calhoun. 240 pp. Overwhelmed, Sara saw only one way out—leaving . . . ISBN 1-59493-030-9 $12.95

TURNING THE TABLES by Jessica Thomas. 240 pp. The 2nd Alex Peres Mystery. *From ghosties and ghoulies and long leggity beasties* . . . ISBN 1-59493-009-0 $12.95

FOR EVERY SEASON by Frankie Jones. 240 pp. Andi, who is investigating a 65-year-old murder, meets Janice, a charming district attorney . . . ISBN 1-59493-010-4 $12.95

LOVE ON THE LINE by Laura DeHart Young. 240 pp. Kay leaves a younger woman behind to go on a mission to Alaska . . . will she regret it? ISBN 1-59493-008-2 $12.95

UNDER THE SOUTHERN CROSS by Claire McNab. 200 pp. Lee, an American travel agent, goes down under and meets Australian Alex, and the sparks fly under the Southern Cross. ISBN 1-59493-029-5 $12.95

SUGAR by Karin Kallmaker. 240 pp. Three women want sugar from Sugar, who can't make up her mind. ISBN 1-59493-001-5 $12.95

FALL GUY by Claire McNab. 200 pp. 16th Detective Inspector Carol Ashton Mystery. ISBN 1-59493-000-7 $12.95

ONE SUMMER NIGHT by Gerri Hill. 232 pp. Johanna swore to never fall in love again— but then she met the charming Kelly . . . ISBN 1-59493-007-4 $12.95

TALK OF THE TOWN TOO by Saxon Bennett. 181 pp. Second in the series about wild and fun loving friends. ISBN 1-931513-77-5 $12.95

LOVE SPEAKS HER NAME by Laura DeHart Young. 170 pp. Love and friendship, desire and intrigue, spark this exciting sequel to *Forever and the Night.* ISBN 1-59493-002-3 $12.95

TO HAVE AND TO HOLD by Peggy J. Herring. 184 pp. By finally letting down her defenses, will Dorian be opening herself to a devastating betrayal? ISBN 1-59493-005-8 $12.95

WILD THINGS by Karin Kallmaker. 228 pp. Dutiful daughter Faith has met the perfect man. There's just one problem: she's in love with his sister. ISBN 1-931513-64-3 $12.95

SHARED WINDS by Kenna White. 216 pp. Can Emma rebuild more than just Lanny's marina? ISBN 1-59493-006-6 $12.95

THE UNKNOWN MILE by Jaime Clevenger. 253 pp. Kelly's world is getting more and more complicated every moment. ISBN 1-931513-57-0 $12.95

TREASURED PAST by Linda Hill. 189 pp. A shared passion for antiques leads to love. ISBN 1-59493-003-1 $12.95

SIERRA CITY by Gerri Hill. 284 pp. Chris and Jesse cannot deny their growing attraction . . . ISBN 1-931513-98-8 $12.95

ALL THE WRONG PLACES by Karin Kallmaker. 174 pp. Sex and the single girl—Brandy is looking for love and usually she finds it. Karin Kallmaker's first *After Dark* erotic novel.

ISBN 1-931513-76-7 $12.95

WHEN THE CORPSE LIES A Motor City Thriller by Therese Szymanski. 328 pp. Butch bad-girl Brett Higgins is used to waking up next to beautiful women she hardly knows. Problem is, this one's dead.   ISBN 1-931513-74-0 $12.95

GUARDED HEARTS by Hannah Rickard. 240 pp. Someone's reminding Alyssa about her secret past, and then she becomes the suspect in a series of burglaries.

ISBN 1-931513-99-6 $12.95

ONCE MORE WITH FEELING by Peggy J. Herring. 184 pp. Lighthearted, loving, romantic adventure.   ISBN 1-931513-60-0 $12.95

TANGLED AND DARK A Brenda Strange Mystery by Patty G. Henderson. 240 pp. When investigating a local death, Brenda finds two possible killers—one diagnosed with Multiple Personality Disorder.   ISBN 1-931513-75-9 $12.95

WHITE LACE AND PROMISES by Peggy J. Herring. 240 pp. Maxine and Betina realize sex may not be the most important thing in their lives.   ISBN 1-931513-73-2 $12.95

UNFORGETTABLE by Karin Kallmaker. 288 pp. Can Rett find love with the cheerleader who broke her heart so many years ago?   ISBN 1-931513-63-5 $12.95

HIGHER GROUND by Saxon Bennett. 280 pp. A delightfully complex reflection of the successful, high society lives of a small group of women.   ISBN 1-931513-69-4 $12.95

LAST CALL A Detective Franco Mystery by Baxter Clare. 240 pp. Frank overlooks all else to try to solve a cold case of two murdered children . . .   ISBN 1-931513-70-8 $12.95

ONCE UPON A DYKE: NEW EXPLOITS OF FAIRY-TALE LESBIANS by Karin Kallmaker, Julia Watts, Barbara Johnson & Therese Szymanski. 320 pp. You've never read fairy tales like these before! From Bella After Dark.   ISBN 1-931513-71-6 $14.95

FINEST KIND OF LOVE by Diana Tremain Braund. 224 pp. Can Molly and Carolyn stop clashing long enough to see beyond their differences?   ISBN 1-931513-68-6 $12.95

DREAM LOVER by Lyn Denison. 188 pp. A soft, sensuous, romantic fantasy.

ISBN 1-931513-96-1 $12.95

NEVER SAY NEVER by Linda Hill. 224 pp. A classic love story . . . where rules aren't the only things broken.   ISBN 1-931513-67-8 $12.95

PAINTED MOON by Karin Kallmaker. 214 pp. Stranded together in a snowbound cabin, Jackie and Leah's lives will never be the same.   ISBN 1-931513-53-8 $12.95

WIZARD OF ISIS by Jean Stewart. 240 pp. Fifth in the exciting Isis series.

ISBN 1-931513-71-4 $12.95

WOMAN IN THE MIRROR by Jackie Calhoun. 216 pp. Josey learns to love again, while her niece is learning to love women for the first time.   ISBN 1-931513-78-3 $12.95

SUBSTITUTE FOR LOVE by Karin Kallmaker. 200 pp. When Holly and Reyna meet the combination adds up to pure passion. But what about tomorrow?   ISBN 1-931513-62-7 $12.95

GULF BREEZE by Gerri Hill. 288 pp. Could Carly really be the woman Pat has always been searching for?   ISBN 1-931513-97-X $12.95

THE TOMSTOWN INCIDENT by Penny Hayes. 184 pp. Caught between two worlds, Eloise must make a decision that will change her life forever.   ISBN 1-931513-56-2 $12.95